Hothead

Love Burns Series: Book Four

Isobel Reed

Hothead
Love Burns Series: Book Four
Copyright © 2025 Isobel Reed
All rights reserved.

ISBN: (ebook) 978-1-964636-33-7
(print) 978-1-964636-34-4

Inkspell Publishing
207 Moonglow Circle #101
Murrells Inlet, SC 29576

Edited By Yezanira Venecia
Cover art By Emily's World By Design

DEDICATION

For the doubters, the cynics, and the skeptics who swore a fuckboy could never become a prince—this one's for you.

ISOBEL REED

CHAPTER ONE

Of all the times Luke could have walked into a door, it had to happen now, didn't it? At the fire station. And he didn't even care that it was in front of all his fellow firefighters. Or that he'd spend the rest of his shift getting the piss taken out of him. No. What mattered was that *she* was there to witness his humiliation. The angel who had just entered the room. The most beautiful woman he'd ever laid eyes on.

Way to go, Cappelli.

"Luke Cappelli?" the woman in question repeated, finally pulling him out of his head.

"Uh, yeah," Luke rasped, his hand shooting up to his forehead to rub what was most likely going to be a big ass bump. "How can I help?"

He watched her take a wary step forward, trying his hardest to keep his expression neutral. The closer she got, the better she looked. And when her silver eyes flashed, he knew he was in trouble.

An errant strand of dirty blonde hair fell to her face as she took her time perusing him. "I'm a friend of your brothers … Well, I *was* a friend."

Wait. What?

"I'm sorry, darlin', you've got the wrong man. I don't have a brother." His eyes began to narrow now. Suspicion

5

not just pulling at his brow. "What did you say your name was?"

She didn't flinch at his denial. Or his tone. It was almost as if she'd expected him to say just that.

Who the hell is this girl?

"My name's Bella." A faint smile began to curve her lips. "I worked with your brother. Well, half brother, I guess. Marco. Marco Cappelli."

He didn't know what was making his stomach churn more, those glittering eyes, that smile, or hearing that name again. After all this time.

Then something clicked. "You said *was ... was a friend*—what does that mean?"

He immediately regretted asking as he witnessed her spark slowly dull and anguish seep into every pore.

Chatter in the background came to a stop. The whole main floor was eerily quiet. So quiet he heard the footsteps of his friends as they began to scatter, pretending to busy themselves. He didn't miss that they were all still very much within earshot.

Nosy bastards.

Another step closer and something that smelled a lot like wild berries hit the back of his throat.

"Marco died. Two months ago," she announced.

His stomach was no longer churning. It was spasming from the punch to the gut he'd just received. Marco was fucking dead? How the hell could he be dead?

You have an audience. Get your shit together.

It was getting harder and harder to think straight. He needed to get out of there before he asked the questions he didn't even know that he wanted answers to. This time his facial expressions weren't neutral, they were blanked as he took another step toward the heavenly being before him, ignoring the berries and closing what little distance was left between them.

"Why are you here?"

Her chin lifted while his dipped. Holy hell. How was it

possible that a woman who had the face of an angel could inspire so much fucking sin? Especially now. Corrupting her is the last thing he should be thinking about.

Talk about not the fucking time. Maybe concentrate on the pounding in your ears first, man?

"Your brother sent me."

"My *dead* brother sent you?" He felt one eyebrow quirk up. "No. Wait. Don't tell me ... you're here to bridge the gap between the living and the dead. Relay a message to me from beyond the grave? All for the bargain price of ninety-nine ninety-five."

His sarcastic reply didn't exactly elicit the reaction he was expecting. Bella's mouth stretched so wide in response that he got his first glimpse of straight white teeth.

Her teeth had to be perfect too, didn't they?

"Marco was right about you."

That jolted him back to reality.

"Look, lady—"

"Bella," she corrected.

"Look, *Bella*, I don't know exactly what Marco told you, but—"

"I have a letter," she cut him off again. Was it him, or did she look like she was enjoying this a bit too much? "He left you a letter."

Luke lost her eyes for a moment as she reached around and pulled out an envelope from her back pocket.

"I don't care if you've got a damn book, lady—"

"Bella," she corrected again.

Seriously? Is this chick for real?

Back was the smile. Oh, she was definitely enjoying this.

Air whooshed in his face as the piece of paper came up. She was waving it, as if that would make him take it.

"You can keep it," he said through gritted teeth. "I don't want it. Like I said earlier, I don't have a brother."

It took all of his willpower to turn on his heel and walk away. But he had to. Needed to. It didn't matter that she was an angel. That she'd managed to stoke a fire in his belly that he'd never felt before. And it definitely didn't matter that she was faking a dramatic sigh behind him. Even if it was award-worthy.

He headed over to the bunks that were off to the left of the main floor. While he may not need sleep, he did need to be alone.

As soon as he shut the door behind him, he let out the breath he'd been holding.

Shit. Marco.

Collapsing into the bottom bunk, he let his head drop into his hands. Marco couldn't have been more than a few years older than him. Late thirties were no age to die. What the hell happened?

Maybe you should have read the letter and found out, dumbass. Or better yet, ask the fucking angel outside.

Speaking of. Just a second later, the door swung open, causing his head to shoot up.

Okay. Maybe she's not outside anymore.

"You always walk away from people mid-conversation, Luke … or am I special?" she scolded.

She was special all right. "You always walk into rooms with big ass *Do Not Enter* signs on them … or am I just lucky?"

A genuine sigh left those sweet red lips, enough to make him regret snapping back. "Look, I get this is hard for you. Believe it or not, I understand. My family are as dysfunctional as they come. Think the Lohans … on meth. So, trust me, I get it."

Seriously, who the hell is this girl?

Rising from the bed, his feet were moving toward her before his brain had a chance to catch up. Only fully registering when nerve endings began lighting up as he sucked down more berries.

Before he knew it, he'd invaded her space. Personal bubble officially popped as his head bowed and their mouths lined up. All it would take was one small dip and he'd know for sure if those lips tasted as sweet as the woman who owned them smelled.

"Why are you here, Bella?"

He noticed her breath quicken. "Marco asked me to come." She rushed out. "To give you the letter and ..."

"And what?"

"And h-he wanted me to stick around for a while."

He ignored the hammering of his heart at her declaration. His body couldn't be trusted.

"And why would he want you to stick around?"

"Are you going to take the letter?"

"You always answer questions with questions?"

Luke felt her breath warm his skin and found himself wishing away his stubble. He wanted to feel her sink into every inch of him.

Yeah. That's normal.

"Is this the proximity you conduct all your conversations?" was her reply.

It looked like he'd met a fellow smartass. The first one to drag a smile out of him.

This chick is something else.

"I'll tell you what, angel"—his grin only grew as her eyebrow raised—"you tell me exactly what Marco told you about me, and I'll take the letter. Then you can go on your merry way back to wherever you came from."

"You got a spare few hours?"

What a stupid question. He made sure his face conveyed as much. "You know I don't. In case you haven't noticed, darlin', I'm at work."

"I guess I'll be sticking around then. Until you have time." With that, she abruptly turned, leaving his body begging for more as her hand met the door handle. "I'm staying at the Evans ranch—come find me when you're ready to talk."

The Evans ranch? For fuck's sake.

***

Luke's friend Zach gave him a wide berth for the rest of his shift, clearly picking up on Luke's "I don't want to talk about it" vibes. While Hunter left without saying a word. It was only Benny who dared to approach Luke, the youngest of their little friendship group.

The default grin that was normally on his friend's face was replaced with something sullener. Serious.

Here we go.

"So ... is it true? Do you have a brother?" Benny decided then to lean against the fire truck. Against the exact spot Luke had just finished cleaning.

This day just gets better and better.

"I really don't wanna talk about it." He puffed, continuing to clean, putting a bit too much weight behind the steel spot he was drying.

"Come on, don't be like that, man. Put yourself in my shoes. You really think that if the roles were reversed and some chick came in and announced I had a brother—a dead one at that—you wouldn't be all over me?"

"Actually, *Zach* would be all over you," Luke corrected. "*I* would mind my own business."

And it was true. Zach was the one always wanting to talk about crap. Hunter was the strong, silent type. And Luke, well, he wasn't interested in talking either. Unless, of course, there was a sarcastic comment to be made or a man to wind up.

"Bullshit," Benny spat. "My long-lost brother turns up dead and you're seriously telling me you wouldn't have shit to say?"

This was one of the problems with having friends. They liked to insert themselves into your business. Whether you liked it or not.

Luke realized then he would need to throw his friend a bone if he had any hope of being left alone. Not too much information. Just enough to get him off his back.

Taking a break from drying, Luke pushed against the truck with both hands, his head dropping between his outstretched arms.

"Fine. Technically, yes, I have a brother. Or *had* one. But I didn't know him. Didn't grow up with him. I met the guy a couple of times. Like twenty years ago. My dad put it about, okay? He had a bad habit of making kids he had no business having. You happy?"

There. He'd done it. Short and to the point. The only way he knew how to be. Not that he did talking about his past very often. In fact, right there was probably the most he'd ever shared out loud before. Taking him to his maximum sharing limit for the day. Quite possibly the year.

When Benny didn't reply, Luke forced his head up, pushing against the steel one last time until he was facing his friend.

"What?" Luke asked as soon as he caught a glimpse of Benny's thoughtful expression.

"It's just ... it's good to hear you talking about this shit, man. We've worked together ... what, five, six years? And never once have I heard you talk about anything real. Like your family or your shithead of a dad."

It was ironic how little Luke had actually shared to get such a reaction out of Benny. That was just the tip of the iceberg when it came to Luke's childhood. But he wasn't about to point that out. Not when his friend seemed somewhat satisfied with his answer.

He nodded then. A silent gesture indicating that was the end of the conversation as he went back to cleaning the truck.

Benny was off his back, now all Luke had to do was stop thinking about the goddamn angel who'd caused all of this commotion. He had a niggling feeling that getting her out of the fire station was the easy part. Getting her out of his life though ... that would be another story.

ISOBEL REED

CHAPTER TWO

Things were not going according to plan. As a matter of fact, things were so far off plan, Bella was already considering storming the fire station again.

Luke Cappelli was supposed to take the letter. Read the goddamn letter. And then ask her questions. Which she would answer as best she could. She'd stick around for a couple of weeks, make sure he was okay, then go back to San Francisco and sort out her life. What he was not supposed to do was deny knowing Marco, refuse the envelope, and then kick her ass out. And he definitely wasn't supposed to make her stomach clench.

Now here she was, two days later, still on the Evans ranch, still waiting for Luke to turn up. Wasting valuable time that could've been spent doing something useful. *Like looking for a job or a place to live?* Exactly. Important things like that. Things she'd lost right along with her best friend two months ago.

Remember you're doing this for him.

With that reminder, she blew out a long breath, her eyes sweeping across the cozy guest cabin she was currently inhabiting. The ranch was nice. And her room was clearly brand new. She'd been practically blinded by the shine when she'd first stepped in.

The views outside are pretty good too.

They were. And Wade Evans, one of the three brothers who ran the ranch, had even been kind enough to take her on a trail ride yesterday. Saving her from climbing the walls. But she couldn't enjoy it. Not really. Not when she'd been sent to Woodvalley Pines for a reason. And every day she wasn't doing what she was supposed to do was a waste.

"This is ridiculous." She was done waiting.

Grabbing her keys and the letter, she pushed open the cabin door and started the walk up to the main house where her car was parked. It was time to pay Luke Cappelli another visit. This time she would not be walking away.

As she grumbled all the way to her Prius, she made sure to recite the plan. A few times. Just in case her body decided to betray her again. Apparently, her libido was ready to make an appearance after a yearlong coma. And it was dumb enough to think it was in charge.

Once she was buckled in, it took just five minutes to make it into town. She was going back to the scene of the crime. The fire station. If Luke wasn't there, she was betting someone there would know where he was.

Taking in the small-town Wyoming sights as she went, she couldn't help but chuckle at what she saw.

Wow. The people of Woodvalley sure do like their antique shops.

But it wasn't the fifth antique shop that she passed that made her look twice this time. It was the diner. Belonging to someone called Molly, if the sign was accurate. There, sat in the window, was a familiar figure. Scruffy brown hair that was well overdue a cut. Black stubble casting a faint shadow on his chin. And a look of doom on his serious face. Luke.

"Gotcha." She grinned.

Slowing down, she scanned the area for a place to park. Luckily for her, there weren't too many people in the market for antiques today, so it didn't take long to find a spot.

Once she was out of the car and marching along the terracotta cobbles, she used the walk to give herself one last talking to. Today, she was not going to get distracted. She was not going to deviate from the plan. And if her stomach started to clench again, she'd order a damn peppermint tea and sort that shit out.

You've got this, Bella.

Pushing through the glass door, she didn't bother surveying the garish bright red room. She knew exactly where Luke was, and that's where she was heading.

His head was down as she approached, and he was staring into his coffee cup like it had the answers to all of life's questions. It wasn't until she slid into the booth seat opposite that he looked up. Well, more like jolted.

"What the—Jesus."

"Bella," she corrected, unable to hide her smile. "But I'll take it."

His dark eyes narrowed on her again. He liked doing that. *Maybe he thinks it's intimidating?* It wasn't.

"So much for me coming to you, huh?" he groused.

His complaint was met with a shrug. "What can I say, I changed my mind. Besides, it's not polite to leave a lady waiting, Cappelli."

He didn't reply. Instead, he took his time considering her. Testing her composure as his eyes dragged over her face, down her neck, across her outfit, and then slowly back up again, leaving a trail of fire in his wake. The way the man looked at her should be illegal. Or at the very least come with a warning sign.

Come on. Think non-sexual thoughts. Sport. Yes, think of a sport. Like, uh, baseball. Um, baseball bats. Baseball jerseys. Huh. What would Luke look like in a baseball jersey? What would Luke look like without a jersey? Goddamnit.

"I've been working." He eventually grunted, oblivious to her internal struggle as her knee began to bounce under the steel countertop. "Night shifts."

Taking a sip of his coffee, his dark brown stare didn't waver. It was doing a damn fine job of holding her in place.

Not helping.

Faking nonchalance and doing pretty well pretending his attention wasn't causing convulsions to near catastrophic levels in her belly, Bella leaned back into the squeaky red cushion.

"So, now that you're not working, I take it you were just on your way over to see me?"

"No, *Bella*, I wasn't."

Even the way he said her name made her skin all tingly. *Pull. Yourself. Together.*

"Then it's a good job I came to *you* then, isn't it?" He didn't answer. Just stared. Holding her eyes hostage and heating her insides.

Stop getting distracted!

Very much needing to put a stop to the air crackling around them, she reached around and pulled Marco's letter from her back pocket and placed it on the table in front of Luke.

Her plan didn't work. The intensity between them only kicked up a notch as his gaze remained fixed on her.

She held firm though. Played his game and stared right back into molten chocolate, ensuring he saw nothing but composed detachment.

One minute later, she quietly congratulated herself as he finally broke the silence.

"What happened to him?" Luke asked, his voice cracking.

Bella straightened. This was it. Why she was here. She just had to get through the next few minutes without letting her own voice crack, or God forbid, letting the tears take over.

Her elbows hit the table as she leaned forward, the determination to do Marco's story justice the only thing keeping her steady. "Your brother was an amazing man. Did you know he won an IDA award?"

"IDA?"

"International Documentary Association." She nodded. "It's one of the most prestigious awards you can receive as a documentary maker."

She could see by Luke's reaction he had no idea Marco

was a filmmaker. Let alone a good one. She shouldn't really be shocked. Luke had denied even having a brother only forty-eight hours ago.

"Okay, well, I guess I should start at the beginning then. He made documentaries. Good ones. I'm ... well, I *was* his cameraman."

He raised an eyebrow at her, a look that shouldn't have been sexy, though on Luke, it was. But she definitely wasn't thinking about how sexy the man was. No. Definitely not. Because that would mean she might possibly deviate from the plan. And there would be no deviating today. None, whatsoever.

"Anyway"—she cleared her throat before continuing—"we were filming out in Florida working on a documentary exploring the roots of the 'Don't Say Gay' bills when it happened."

Suddenly, she felt sick. And it wasn't the good kind from a minute ago. It was the "holy shit, bile is coming up" kind. So much for the cool composure she'd worked so hard to maintain. Her knee was back to bouncing, and her palms had started to sweat.

"Uh, I think I need a drink before I go any further. Don't suppose Molly's got a stash of hard liquor behind the counter?"

Those curious eyes were on the move again. Searching out her expression, looking for what, she had no idea. Then, he surprised her.

"The hardest drink you're gonna get here, angel, is an ice cream float." She figured as much. "But I've got a bottle of whiskey back at mine, if you're interested?"

Did he really just say that? He'd gone full frigging circle. Denial. Dismissal. Avoidance. To a goddamn invitation. To his home of all places. And he had to go and call her angel again while he did it, didn't he?

But there was no time to overanalyze; she had whiskey to drink and a story to tell.

"Let's go."

***

Luke's place was not the hovel she'd originally imagined. It was actually pretty frigging nice. She'd go as far as to say it was a little bit fancy. It was a house too, not an apartment. Again, not what she was expecting.

Of course it had the bachelor essentials, like a ginormous flat screen and huge black leather sofas. But what surprised her most was the décor. Everything was minimal. Neat. And completely spotless. She was scared to touch anything in case she left a fingerprint.

He must have a cleaner. No man is this tidy.

Deciding the safest place to be was seated, she made her way over to one of the couches. Her eyes darted to the coffee table as she perched down, which resembled a huge traveling trunk. It even looked like it opened. She was tempted to find out, her fingers even shooting out to run along the metal seam.

"It doesn't open," Luke rumbled as he re-entered the room, this time with the whiskey bottle he'd promised and two tumblers. "That would be far too practical."

He wasted no time bouncing down next to her and pouring out the honey-hued liquid. She found herself twisting to look at him, her eyes roaming from the bottle, all the way up his arm to the bulging bicep threatening to spill from his T-shirt. When she eventually came to his chiseled chin, his head was turned, a wry smile on his face as he offered her a glass.

"Why a trunk?" she asked, accepting the drink and almost too enthusiastically taking a big gulp.

"Why not a trunk?" That smile grew much wider than she thought possible. And it changed his whole face. Lit it up until there was an actual glow.

Jesus Christ, Bella. You've had one sip, stop acting like a drunk moron.

Her mental scolding didn't work. She continued to act

like a drunk moron. One with nothing to say, because she was too busy admiring that freaking glow.

"So," he prompted, "hard liquor has been officially administered … you ready to tell me what happened now?"

No. "Yeah." She downed her drink, relishing the sting as it began warming her insides. She needed all the liquid courage goodness.

Once she was done, and clinking the glass back onto the trunk table, she caught another raised eyebrow. And ignored it.

"So, Florida." She nodded to herself, not sure if it was the memories or the whiskey burning her chest. "He had this contact, one who didn't want his identity revealed in the film, which isn't really an issue … we normally only film shadows of them talking and then dub the voice …" *You're getting off track.* "Anyway, the dude was skittish, didn't even want another person in the room when he was interviewed, which meant Marco had to go. Alone." Back was the bile. This time whiskey-flavored.

She needed a minute. Why was this so hard? It had been two months for God's sake. And she'd traveled all the way to Woodvalley Pines for the sole purpose of talking about it. Fulfilling Marco's wishes. Doing the bare minimum compared to what he'd done for her.

"S-Sorry," she stuttered, well aware she'd frozen.

A hand came down and covered hers. But it wasn't the comfort it was intended for that she felt. It was a spark. Something high voltage. Like some sort of live wire coursing through her veins.

I know *that's not normal.*

It didn't make sense. None of her body's reactions did. Luke Cappelli was so not her type. He was cold. So blunt it was bordering on rude. And everything he said was drenched in sarcasm. Sure, he was easy on the eye, but other than that, there was nothing remotely charming about him.

Except when he calls you angel.

No. She needed to stop this madness now. She did not

come all the way to Woodvalley to hook up with Marco's brother. That would be beyond fucked up. Even for her.

"It's okay, angel, take your time."

Urgh. Fuck my life.

If only for the distraction of their joined hands, which now seemed to be throbbing, she allowed herself to go back to that night. The night that changed everything.

"Uh, yeah, so the interview. Like a dumbass, I let him go on his own. I realized only after he left that I didn't have an address for him either. Which wasn't like Marco at all. We've been to some scary ass places together, so safety was always top of our list. We would hardly ever go anywhere alone. And on the very few occasions we did, our phone trackers would be on, addresses would be shared, and times would be agreed beforehand." She paused to take a deep breath. The guilt threatening to choke her.

Now is not the time.

Her inner voice was right. Now was not the time to berate herself again. It was too late. There was no going back to fix this. She needed to accept that.

The hand on her squeezed, reminding her that she had an audience, one who was probably wondering why she'd stopped talking.

"I don't know what happened this time." Her voice was much quieter when she spoke again. "Why it was different. Maybe it was 'cause the guy was skittish or maybe it was just a fuck-up from our end … but either way, it happened. And he was off the radar for a long time."

Letting her eyes flutter shut, everything from that night began to overwhelm her senses. She could still smell that musty old motel room she was holed up in. Still see the flashing blue and red neon from the police cars bouncing off the walls. And then there was the robotic, monotone sound of Detective Hardy's voice that rang in her ears as he shattered Bella's heart with just one word.

"He killed Marco," she whispered. Her vision still cloaked in blackness. "The guy he went to interview. He wasn't skittish. Or scared for his life. He was a fucking hunter. And Marco was his prey."

CHAPTER THREE

Bella looked like she was about to hurl, and Luke couldn't blame her. He felt like hurling too. This was some seriously messed up shit. A goddamn real-life horror show. One he was struggling to get his head around.

Turning Bella's hand until her palm was facing upward, he laced their fingers together and gave her another squeeze. What he was dying to do was pull her into his arms. Hold her tight. Tell her everything was going to be okay. But that was just freaking crazy. He'd known the woman five minutes and his screwed-up brain was acting like she was his. He didn't even want to think about what his body was doing.

Then something she said clicked. "You said Marco was prey … how so? Why would this guy go after him?"

Those beautiful bright eyes shot open and were back on him. "Marco was gay. That's why he was killed."

What the fucking fuck?

Every muscle in Luke's body tightened, even the one gripping Bella's hand. "W-what?"

"He was gay," she repeated, eyeing him warily.

The anger burning his insides was making it hard to breathe. "You're saying some fucker hunted Marco down and fucking killed him 'cause of his goddamn sexuality?"

She gave him a solemn nod as moisture pooled in her silver eyes. The sight alone was enough to simmer his rage.

It also made him want to listen to his instincts and pull her into his hold. But he held back.

"Please fucking tell me they caught the guy."

Okay. Maybe the rage is still seething.

It was her turn to squeeze his hand, offering him something he wasn't used to. "They caught him. I had access to Marco's computer. He'd been corresponding with the guy for months, and Marco kept everything. It took a few weeks, but eventually they managed to track the guy down through an IP address."

Thank God for that. That was something at least. And saved Luke from a murder charge of his own.

Lock that shit down.

Emotion was off-limits. It always had been, and it always would be. That Pandora's box was sealed shut, and not even Marco could pry it open. No, instead, Luke would bury today with all the other crap life had thrown his way. At least that was the plan. Until he got a look at the despair dripping down Bella's cheeks.

Without thinking, he tugged on her hand until she fell forward. He wrapped his arms around her, pulling her close and holding her tight as she melted into him.

Luke was not a hugger. Never had been. On the rare occasion he'd been forced to hug another person, it had been awkward at best. Even after sex, he didn't hug. He got the hell out of there and never looked back. So, to hug someone now, of his own accord, was batshit freaking crazy. The fact that he was enjoying every second of it too, made him wonder if hell had frozen over.

What on earth was it about this woman that had him in knots? Made him question what he wanted?

It's just 'cause she's hot. That has to be it. I wanna sleep with her, that's all. End of story.

But when those dainty fingers curled around him and flexed over his back muscles, he was starting to wonder if it was just the beginning.

By the time she pulled back, his mental tug-of-war was

far from over.

"I see you, Luke Cappelli." She looked so deep into him, for a moment, he believed her. "You may have built those bricks around you high, but there is more than one way through a wall."

Who the fuck is this girl?

If there was a wall, then she sure knew how to activate its defences. Denial was his weapon of choice.

"This ain't an after-school special, darlin'—one hug doesn't mean you know me. Far from it. Trust me when I tell you a pretty girl rubbing against me is no hardship. I've got something else you can rub against too if you want?"

Wow. You really just said that, huh?

There was no taking it back now anyway, so he might as well just go with it. Back to being a bastard. A persona he was comfortable with. It had nothing at all to do with what Bella saw in him. Nope. None whatsoever.

He didn't know what he expected her reaction to be. Offended. Embarrassed. God knows he deserved a slap. But her lips tilting up to one side was not it. Flashing him a crooked smile that made her look even more like the fallen angel she was.

"And what exactly did you want me to rub up against, Cappelli?" She must be calling his bluff. Surely?

"Oh, darlin', if you don't know … then I'm more than happy to show you." Never one to shy away from a challenge, he leaned back into the leather, his legs dropping open.

He'd underestimated her though. He realized that as soon as she rose, only to drop back down onto his lap, her legs going wide as she straddled him and laid her hands atop his shoulders.

"By all means … show me." That devilish glint in her eye was enough to make him gulp.

This was going to get embarrassing real quick. There are certain things a man cannot hide when a hot as fuck woman sits right on it.

"Angel," he practically growled at her, "you better make a decision real fast 'cause once you climb on, I expect you to stay for the whole damn ride."

She did not give two shits about his new predicament. It only seemed to spur her on more, moving that sexy ass in his lap until spots behind his eyes started to appear. But it wasn't that which made him want to beg for mercy, no, it was when her head dipped and those red lips drifted over his mouth. Careful not to touch him. Instead, she teased. Whiskey-flavored sugar so close he could taste it.

"Let me guess ... this ride of yours is guaranteed to make me scream?"

"Damn fucking right it is." His hands went to her waist, hauling her closer.

A moment later, he felt the vibration of her hum against his lips, forcing his breathing to pick up. If she carried on like this, he'd be hyperventilating in no time.

He tried to think back to the last time he wanted a woman so badly. And he came up blank. The answer was never. He'd never wanted a woman as badly as he wanted this one.

It wasn't because he needed sex either, which, coincidently, he did. All the anger, unfairness, and regret had to go somewhere. And as far as outlets go, sex had always been a damn fine option. But it was more than that this time. Bella was more than that.

All the more reason to stop right fucking now.

He couldn't even if he wanted to. Especially when those sexy lips dragged up his jawline, grazing his stubble and filling his stomach with fire. When they reached his ear, he felt goosebumps immediately break out across his exposed skin as her breath hit.

"What if I want to make *you* scream, Cappelli?" Did he actually just quiver? The tip of her tongue traced the shell of his ear. He was dangerously close to begging now. For what though, he still wasn't sure. "Such a shame you're not ready for me." *What? Like hell I'm not.* "Not ready for me to run my tongue over every inch of this body, until it's my name you're screaming. Over. And over. And over again."

Jesus H. Christ.

Her hips rocked, and those naughty teeth nipped hard enough to wrench a groan from the depths of his soul.

"I beg to differ, darlin'. You wanna make me scream? You go on right ahead." He had a feeling it wouldn't take long.

Just as he was ready to throw her down and teach that mouth of hers a lesson, he lost her. Her teeth unclasped his abused lobe, her hot body was no longer warming his lap, and her sexy as fuck eyes flared from a new position. Above. Standing next to the couch and looking down.

"Read the letter, Luke." The familiar piece of paper was pulled from her pocket and tossed onto the table. "My number's on the back. Call me when you're ready to stop playing games."

Before he'd had a chance to reply, or even compose himself, she gave him her back—a fine back it was at that—and swayed those hips right on out of his door.

What the hell just happened?

***

It was several hours before Luke did in fact read the letter his brother had left him. And when he did, he couldn't believe what he was reading. So much so, he read it again. And again. And then one more time.

Now he was parked up at the Evans ranch trying to figure out why he'd driven all the way out there. Why his first instinct had been to go to her. She was dangerous. This afternoon had proved that.

Sexual attraction he could handle, the other feelings she was stirring up, however, were another story. It was way out of his comfort zone. And what scared him most, was he had no idea how she'd managed to elicit such a reaction.

She may have thought he was playing games, but he

wasn't. He didn't *want* to want her. He just didn't know how not to. Which was bad enough. But the ultimate head fuck was that it wasn't just his body that craved her. For the first time in his life, he needed more than just the physical. Sure, stripping her naked and taking her sounded like a good time, but discovering more about who she was, what she liked, and who she loved sounded a hell of a lot better.

What the hell is wrong with you, man? You stumble into a Hallmark fucking film or something?

He was cracking up. Clearly.

It's the shock. Grief. The guilt. Marco's gone.

Yes. That was it. He nodded to himself. That had to be it. Hearing Marco's name, learning he'd been murdered, reading his letter, all of it. It had messed with his head. Brought up old wounds that had corrupted the attraction he was feeling for this woman.

He'd decided long ago relationships were not for him. And Bella ... well, he knew from the very first time she shut down the crap he liked to pull, she wasn't the kind of woman you don't walk away from. She's the type you want in your bed every night. To wake up to every day. And who deserved more than what he could give her.

Stop feeling sorry for yourself and make a damn decision.

Right. He needed to get his act together. Fast.

"Fuck it." Creaking open his car door, he pushed out and let his boots crunch the gravel.

He needed answers. That's why he was there. At least that was what he told himself as he stomped down toward the guest cabins, huffing and puffing as he went.

This is not how I expected to be spending my evening.

Night had fallen a while ago, the last of the light long filtered from the sky. Making it hard to see. He supposed he could pull his phone out if he got desperate. For now, he would stick to the path Wade had carved out.

A few minutes later, an orange glow was in sight, illuminating a small wooden cabin. The only one in a row of five that was lit up.

Bella.

It only took one knock, and the door was swung wide.

She was wearing far less than he was prepared for. Tiny peach-colored silk shorts and a matching camisole.

Jesus Christ, she's not wearing a bra. Why does God fucking hate me?

It was something she seemed to notice at the same time as him, as she quickly crossed her arms over her chest, giving him time to put his tongue back in his head.

"Uh ..." She seemed just as tongue-tied for a second, before fixing her face and narrowing those piercing eyes on him. "I thought I told you to call?"

Nice to know her sass was still firmly in place, pajamas on or not.

"Yeah. I didn't want to," he grunted out.

"Oh, well, that clears that up," she mocked, rolling her eyes and taking a step back so he could enter. "I'm gonna go put ... I'll be back in a minute, okay?"

Bella scurried into the bedroom and shut the door, leaving Luke standing in the cabin's main room. A living slash dining room slash kitchen. Small but cozy. Deciding to take a seat on the equally small fabric couch, he dropped his head back against the cushion and let his eyes shut.

You're doing the right thing. You need to know.

When Bella re-entered, he noticed that she was still wearing the shorts, but the vest had been replaced with an oversized band T-shirt. She also happened to be wearing a bra now. Not that he was looking.

"Do you want a drink? I guess it's a bit late for coffee ... Oh! I could make us some hot cocoa?" Just the idea of hot cocoa seemed to light her up. She was practically bouncing. So happy that it made him think twice about declining.

"Sure, angel, hot cocoa sounds good."

Another beam was sent his way as she busied herself behind the counter, his eyes following every move as his brain chastised him for being such a sap.

When she finally came to join him on the couch, hot

chocolate was pushed in front of him, and he had to admit it smelled fricking good. A bit like her.

"Thanks." He accepted the mug and took his first sip.

"So, I take it you read the letter?"

When his attention returned to her, she was twisting on the sofa to face him, pulling her legs up and crossing them over each other.

"Yeah, angel, I did."

"That's it? Please don't tell me you came all the way over here just to grunt at me?"

How she managed to pull a smile out of him so easily, he didn't know. "No, Bella, I didn't come all the way over here to *grunt at you*. I have questions. The first one being … did *you* read the letter?"

It was his turn to twist in his seat now, letting his own leg bend and rest on the cushion.

"No, Luke, of course I didn't. That letter was intended for you and you only." She seemed to be genuinely offended.

He didn't regret asking though. He needed to know. Considering the content. "Okay, fine. How exactly did you meet my brother? Just through work?"

"He's your brother now?" He simply shrugged at her dig. "Okay. Fine. I met *your brother* a long time ago. When I was living on the street. He was working on his first solo documentary, and he asked if he could interview me."

She was living on the goddamn street?

She said it so matter-of-factly. No emotion. Nothing. As if it wasn't a big deal. It was a huge fucking deal. He must have blinked a few too many times because she took pity on him and elaborated.

"It's not a big deal, and no, I don't want to talk about it. But I will tell you about your brother. Anything you want to know. Like I said before, he was an amazing man. I wouldn't be here today if it wasn't for him. I owe him everything."

What does that mean?

Damnit. Maybe he was wrong. Maybe he couldn't do

this. He could feel the pulse in his neck thumping. Surely that wasn't a normal thing to feel?

Bella's hand came to him, landing on his thigh as she leaned forward, offering him the same comfort he'd offered her earlier that day. Only doing it better.

"Why now?" Luke ground out. "Why not come to me a year ago … five years ago … ten? Why write this creepy ass death letter and have you hand deliver it to me? I mean, the guy was thirty-seven for fucks sake, it's not like he was sitting around waiting to die … not like he knew some psycho killer was gonna get him. I just don't get it."

He watched as her hand lifted and began fiddling with the hem of her shorts. He wasn't going to let himself think about how much he missed her touch though.

"You're right, thirty-seven is no age to be preparing for your death. But … you have to understand that because of what he did, he put himself in dangerous situations. A lot. And y'know, there was this one time that we both got shot and I think—"

His scramble across the cushions cut her off. That and his hand cupping her face, lifting it all the way up until he was looking into silver again. "You got fucking shot?"

She didn't speak, just nodded. Her eyes roamed his face with a curiosity he'd not seen before.

"Who the hell shot you?"

"Uh, well." She batted her eyelashes at him then. Like they were talking about the weather and not her almost fucking dying. "We were in the Central African Republic, and we may have accidentally ended up in the middle of a shootout between rebels and security forces."

Who is this woman?

"Central African Republic," he repeated. Not even sure why. It was like his brain was melting. "You *accidentally* ended up in the middle of a shootout?"

Another nod. "It's not like we planned to get shot, Luke. We're not idiots."

Oh, well. That's fine then.

Fucking hell.

"I'm gonna have to take your word for that, angel." He realized then that his hand was still on her, thumbing an impossibly silky cheek. But he didn't move it. He just kept gliding. "Where were you shot?"

His eyes followed her movement as her fingers trailed along her left side. "Here. I was lucky, the bullet skimmed my side, so other than a gnarly scar, it wasn't too bad. Marco, though ... he got shot in the leg. That was bad."

His hand dropped from her face to her waist, a single digit slowly dragging her top up. She should have stopped him; he had no right to see and no right to touch her. But she didn't. She kept her eyes on him. Even as his gaze dipped, he could feel the heat of her stare.

Letting his finger glide over the darkened skin and dip into the curve, he felt his heart speed up. He didn't understand what was happening. But somehow he knew it was something he wasn't equipped to handle. Which was enough to jolt him into action.

Pulling his hand back, he abruptly stood, swallowing hard as he got his first look at her confused expression.

"I have to go," he announced. Not waiting for a reply, he went straight to the door and let himself out, shaking his head the whole way back to the car.

CHAPTER FOUR

Bella was still reeling from last night.

I mean, what the hell was that?

Luke Cappelli was a big, stupid jerk. One tiny little scar and he's out of there faster than the speed of light. Talk about being a shallow asshole.

A knock on the cabin door gave her fury a momentary break. Forcing herself off the couch, where she was currently eating her feelings, she took the three steps to the wooden frame and pulled the door open.

"Hey, Bella." It was Wade. Tipping his cream cowboy hat and flashing her those famous dimples.

"Hey, Wade, what's up?"

Please don't have Cheeto dust on my face.

"Just checking up on you, darlin'. There's a few more folks coming in today, so you'll have some new neighbors. Just wondering if you wanted to join them on some of the activities they've got booked in?"

This was the problem with booking to stay on a ranch. Activities. There was no doubt in her mind that most people visiting the Evans ranch came for the authentic ranch life experience. They wanted trail rides, fishing, and hikes. But not her. She was there for the peace and quiet.

Sure you are. You gonna squeeze that in before or after you relive the hardest time of your life with your best friend's brother?

Stupid brain. She was quick to shake her head in an attempt to rid herself from the troll inside it, and wiped her mouth just in case there was Cheeto dust on it. To be safe.

"I guess I'm not your typical guest, huh?"

"Not sure we've been up and running long enough to have a typical guest." The hat came off as Wade pushed his fingers through dark blond hair. "I just wanna make sure you've got everything you need."

God, he was a sweetheart. If only she had a thing for cowboys. Would sure be easier than lusting over an emotionally unavailable fuckboy.

"To be honest, I'm not really an activity kinda girl. I booked this place mainly 'cause it's in the middle of nowhere and I knew it would be quiet. And I could sure use a whole lot of quiet right now. It's been a really rough couple of months."

Concern was now furrowing his brow. Maybe she'd said too much.

"The reason I came down here was to see someone actually," she was quick to add. Mostly because he looked like he was about to pull out the number for the Samaritans. "Luke. Luke Cappelli. Don't suppose you know him?"

Wade didn't even attempt to hide his shock. "Uh, sure, I know Luke. He's friends with my brother. They work together."

"But I thought Matt and Jonah worked here with you?"

"They do, my older brother Zach, though, he works with Luke."

"Oh." What else was there to say? It was the charm of the small town, she guessed.

"Actually, Zach is up at the main house now with his fiancée, Libby. You wanna come up? Grab some lunch with us?"

Well, eating isn't technically an activity, and she'd proved this morning that she could definitely eat.

"Sure, let me get changed and I'll come up."

***

Libby was sweet. She wasn't an activity person either, so they bonded over that straight away. Libby's idea of a good time was a quiet night in. Bella totally got it. If she had a man who was looking at her the way Zach was looking at Libby, there's no way in hell she'd want to leave the house either.

Zach seemed like a nice guy too. Relaxed. Friendly. Open. Not at all like Luke. Bella even had trouble imagining them as friends. They were total opposites.

Stop thinking about Luke.

Right. Easier said than done. Especially when the people she was currently breaking bread with at the Evans' dining table were eyeing her with the same curiosity and suspicion Luke had. They were doing it a lot more subtly though. Way more politely. But it didn't change the fact that the reason she was there was the big elephant in the room.

"Okay, I'm gonna ask," Libby announced, leaving Wade and Zach to shake their heads in disapproval. Figures that she was the only one with balls in the room. "Other than to let Luke know about his brother passing … what else brings you here? I mean, what are your plans now that you've told him?"

Bella swallowed down another sip of her diet soda before she answered, feeling rather uncomfortable under the spotlight as all eyes turned to her.

"Well, Luke's brother, Marco … he was my best friend. My only friend, really." *Did you really have to tell them that? Way to sound like a loser.* "Anyway, so, as his best friend, it's kind of my duty to carry out his final wishes, right? Right. So one of those wishes was that I stay on in Woodvalley for a bit after speaking with his brother. So that's what I'm doing." She shrugged. "I guess he wanted me to have a vacation."

That was mostly the truth. Minus the whole promise to keep an eye on Luke and make sure he was okay before leaving. Although, the way everyone was looking at her, you'd think she was trying to convince them all that the Pope wasn't catholic.

"A vacation?" Zach's head tilted with the question.

"Yep."

Libby's mouth opened as if she was about to ask something else, but she was silenced by the sound of dirt being kicked up outside.

Everyone's attention whipped to the window, including hers. The car wasn't very interesting, but the man who stepped out of it managed to quicken her pulse. Luke. A pissed-off-looking Luke.

She was up and out the backdoor before she knew what she was doing. As soon as her boots hit gravel, Luke's neck twisted her way.

He didn't look surprised. Or any less pissed.

"Why now?" he shouted, distress marring every wrinkle on his face. "Why wait until *now?*"

She hadn't realized the others had followed her outside until she heard Wade clear his throat behind her.

"Reign it in, Luke," Wade warned.

She turned to her host and offered him a placating smile. "It's okay. Do you mind giving us a minute?"

Wade looked back at Luke and took a moment to consider before eventually nodding. But he didn't look happy. Zach and Libby didn't look any happier as they followed suit and left Bella and Luke alone.

Bella's attention was back on the man in question as soon as the door slammed closed. Rage and despair had morphed into one.

This is why you're here, remember? You can do this.

Trying not to spook him, she slowly edged forward. When she was confident that he wouldn't protest, she grabbed his hand and tugged.

"Come on, I think I can help." Leading him to her car, she opened the passenger side and gestured him in. Shockingly, he didn't put up a fight.

Slumped into the leather seat, it was only when they were

driving through the valley that he actually spoke again. "Where are we going?"

"You'll see."

"I'm pissed." He felt the need to clarify.

"I noticed."

"I don't get it. Why write me a letter with this shit instead of picking up the fucking phone? What's the point of waiting until he's dead to do this ... when I can't do a goddamn thing about it?"

She understood his frustration. She really did. And while she'd not read the letter in question, she had a good idea about some of the contents. "I can't answer that, Luke. I don't know." She sighed. "Maybe he thought he had time. Who knows?"

Taking a turn down an old dirt road, she waited until they were close to the treeline before parking up. On her first day in Woodvalley, she'd stumbled upon this very spot. And it was perfect for what she had in mind.

Stepping out of the car, she felt Luke's eyes burn into her, but he didn't say anything. So she waited. Staring back until he reluctantly rounded the vehicle. Once he was within touching distance, she took hold of his hand again, ignoring the warm tug in her belly as she did so. Pulling, or more like dragging him along, she walked them into the midst of the forest until they were surrounded by nothing but tall oaks.

"Is this where you chop me up and I end up on one of those true crime shows?" Luke cast an eye over the area before pinning her with a suspicious stare.

"Not yet. But another few days of you and your charming personality and all bets are off." She smirked, feeling a tiny bit satisfied as his glare cracked into a wonky smile.

"You gonna tell me why you brought me here, angel?"

God. He really needed to stop calling her that.

"I brought you here so you could let it all out. Everything you've been holding onto. Scream. Shout. Curse the universe. Just get that shit out of your system. There's no judgment here. It's just me, you, and the trees."

"Are you being serious?"

"Yep. Trust me, it'll make you feel better." She could tell he wasn't convinced.

"And you do this? You come here and scream?"

"Well, not here, *technically*. But I have done it, if that's what you're asking. Not every day, I'm not a total psycho … but I'm not ashamed to admit that I occasionally enjoy cursing the universe pretty damn loudly."

"You're fucking insane."

She shrugged. "Maybe. Maybe not. You're curious though, right?"

Luke was quiet for a while, his eyes no longer scanning their surroundings but firmly on her. A lesser woman might crumble under his scrutiny, but not her. She'd been steel-enforced for a long time; it would take a lot more than Luke Cappelli to break her.

"Okay, fine. You first, though. Show me how it's done."

"Okay." She didn't even hesitate to agree. He wrongly thought this would be a way to get out of doing it. "And you promise you'll give it a go?"

"I promise."

Turning away from him, she took a few steps forward and tipped back her head. In an instant, a resounding scream was ripping through her and bouncing off the trees.

God, that felt good.

It had been a while since she screamed into the abyss. She needed it a lot more than she realized. Especially now that she'd lost Marco. The universe had a lot to answer for. And she had yet another thing to scream about.

By the time she turned to walk back to Luke, her muscles felt looser and her mind calmer. He didn't look any less tense though, but some fire had returned to his eyes. His crooked smile still tipped his lips.

"Your turn."

He didn't reply, just strode toward her. His gaze was glued to her. She only lost his stare when he passed her, taking her screaming spot. Deciding to give him some space, she stepped back a bit further.

It must have been a whole minute before he made good on his promise. Roaring into the undergrowth. But she could tell he was holding back. A short, sharp shriek wasn't going to cut it. Not when he was carrying around a lifetime of rage.

"Again," she yelled.

Another howl erupted. This one louder. Enough to shake the trees. He was getting closer.

"Again."

The next one sounded like it had been torn straight from his soul. A hoarse cry, which was still ringing in her ears as he dropped to his knees, his head next to follow as he cradled it in his hands.

That's more like it.

She went to him then, thumping onto the ground next to him and shuffling closer until she could wrap her hands around his waist. He came willingly into her hold. His head resting on her shoulder as his own arms curled around her body.

Bella had no idea how long they stayed like that. In the quiet. With only the sounds of their breaths mingling and the birds singing. But right now, she knew she needed this just as much as he did. Grief was one hell of a motherfucker.

***

The journey back to the ranch was super quiet. Luke was clearly pissed he'd let his mask slip, even if it was only for a short while.

Bella had a feeling he wasn't as good at hiding as he thought he was, though. She'd known him ... what, a couple of days? And already he'd shown her a lot more of himself than she suspected, he showed anyone else.

By the time Luke slammed the passenger door shut, she was thankful for the reprieve. The intensity inside her Prius was almost suffocating. She was fairly certain a minute longer in the car and she would have choked.

It was only after she'd gulped down a lung full of fresh air that she noticed the normally deserted gravel around the main house was unusually full ... of cars.

As if on cue, Wade and several people she didn't recognize began filing out of the front door.

"Bella!" Wade waved, changing his direction and leading the group over toward Luke and her.

Putting on her happy, friendly face, she tried for a smile. Well aware she had Luke's full attention. Even with a whole car between them, she still felt those dark eyes sink into her skin.

"Glad we caught you," Wade started even before he'd finished closing the distance. "Bella, I'd like you to meet your new neighbors. Guys, this is Bella, another guest on the ranch."

For some reason, her brain decided a dorky wave would be appropriate. It was too late to stop it now. She was already waving and trying her best not to grimace at the group.

"I'm Calvin." A man who looked like he couldn't be too much older than her broke free from the herd to shake her hand.

"Hi, Calvin, nice to meet you." She attempted a warm smile, but her mouth wasn't cooperating.

What's with me today?

She didn't even know why she was bothering to ask herself that when the answer was obvious. Luke. Luke, who was saddling up next to her.

But his presence or the scowl he was giving poor old Calvin wasn't the strangest thing to happen, not when you compare it to what happened next. Luke's hand shot out and curved around her waist. And pulled. Until she was tucked into his side.

"Oh, uh, is this your husband?" Calvin asked, looking a little sheepish.

The snort she emitted wasn't the most ladylike. But who the hell cared.

"Uh, no, this is not my *husband*." She took a moment to glare at Luke before turning back to Calvin. "This is Luke. A *friend*."

Luke scoffed then, tightening his grip on her hip.

"Okay." Wade clapped his hands, likely attempting to break the tension. "Well, we just wanted to say hi. And don't forget, if you wanna join these guys on any of the excursions they've got booked, just give me a shout. Oh, and I expect to see you at the barbecue on Friday." He flashed her those dimples again. Damn. She'd forgotten she'd already agreed to go to that.

"We'll be there." Luke nodded at Wade and then to Calvin.

Will we?

This guy was giving her whiplash with these mood swings.

As Wade directed the guests back the way they came, she attempted to turn, mostly to shoot daggers directly into Luke's eyes, but it was harder than she thought, especially with his big hand still on her in a vice-like grip.

When she did eventually manage to twist in his hold, she was far too close to him and his dumb intoxicating peppery leather scent that she was in no way enjoying breathing in.

"*We* will be there?" She wasn't going to let the flecks of black in his eyes distract her. No, siree.

"Yup." He was giving her nothing. No smile. No frown. No nothing. Just a blank and mildly infuriating stare.

"*Yup?*" she repeated, no longer hiding her annoyance. "I take it that means you're not done with your questions if you're gonna grace me with your presence again?"

"Nope."

Well, okey dokey then.

"Right." She nodded, mostly in frustration. "Well, as much as I'm enjoying the scintillating conversation we've got going on here, I need to go eat ... so I'm gonna go. I guess I'll see you at the barbecue."

"That's it?"

"Uh, yeah. What were you expecting?" She threw him a puzzled look.

"I've got steaks back at my place."

"Great. I'm happy for you." She managed to cross her arms and quirk her hip. The hip he just so happened to still be holding on to.

"Angel." He sighed, shaking his head as if she was the infuriating one. "Do you like steak?"

"Why? You gonna recommend a local butcher?"

She was able to crack that impassive expression again. It was only a lip twitch, but she'd take it.

"No, angel, I'm trying to invite you to dinner."

"Oh."

"Yeah, oh." Was it just her imagination, or was his thumb stroking her waist now? "Well? What do you say?"

I'm thinking, I'm thinking. Don't rush me.

Maybe it was the leather filling her lungs. Or the brush of his thumb on her exposed skin. Or maybe it was because he was currently looking at her like he was dying of thirst, and she was a tall drink of water. Whatever it was that made her say yes, she said it. And soon she'd have to live with the consequences.

CHAPTER FIVE

Like a dumbass, Luke had invited Bella over for dinner. *Why the hell did I do that again?*

Who was he kidding, he knew exactly why. He still wanted her. Worse than before. As if that were even possible. And seeing that douchebag Calvin practically drool all over her had obviously short-circuited Luke's brain. Made him make questionable choices.

Now here he was in his kitchen, flipping steaks and pretending like this wasn't a big fucking deal. Well, it was. Not once in thirty-five years had he made dinner for a woman. He hadn't even taken one out to a restaurant. Luke Cappelli did not date.

If he wanted a woman, he picked her up in a bar, normally out of town, went back to her place, and then disappeared before sunlight. That might make him a dick, but that was who he was. No strings. No commitment. No fuss.

Nothing like what was going on now. Actually, he had no idea what the hell was going on. But one thing was for sure, it reeked of complication.

Being all new to this, he was struggling with how to handle the unfamiliar feelings bubbling to the surface. Never before had he simply wanted to just be with a woman. No ulterior motives. No plans to get her naked. Just being in her company because he enjoyed it. Craved it.

The more time he spent with her, the stronger the pull between them became. There was no one thing that made him feel this way. It was all of it. The way their personalities seemed to click, her dark sense of humor, and the sharp sarcasm she effortlessly threw out. He wanted more of everything. He wanted more of her.

You're so fucked.

He was. That was made obvious when Bella strolled up to the marble counter beside him and jumped up onto the surface, swinging her legs until she was intermittently kicking his thigh. But it wasn't his legs he was worried about. It was the ache in his chest that had formed at just the sight of her.

"So, what's up with the fancy ass pad, Cappelli?"

"Excuse me?" He stole another glance just as she was flicking her wild waves over one shoulder.

"This place. It's a little big for a bachelor, don't you think? And don't even get me started on the designer décor. I'm scared to touch anything in case I break something I can't afford."

He rolled his eyes at that as he opened the cupboard to pull out some plates. "And yet here you are, sitting on my kitchen counter without a care in the world."

"True. Guess I better run the numbers. What did this marble set you back?" she asked as her hand teasingly skimmed over the surface.

Plating up the food, he felt his head shake and a smile break. How was she doing this? He didn't even smile this often around his friends.

"I'll have to get back to you on that—it's time to eat, angel."

When he looked back, she was smiling too. A smile so bright it lit up her whole face.

Goddamn, she's beautiful.

He needed to focus. Food. Right. They were going to eat. Taking the plates to the table he'd set up on the patio, he used the walk over as an opportunity to try and sort himself out. He heard Bella jump down and follow behind, but he didn't dare look back as he passed through the sliding doors.

"Very nice," Bella declared as she pulled out a chair.

That was another thing. He'd purposely spent time trying to make the table look nice for her. He'd even put a candle out. A freaking candle?!

Who even am I?

"Why do you look pissed off?"

Perfect. He wasn't even shutting down his facial expressions around her anymore.

"I'm not pissed off." Okay, even he could admit that didn't sound all too convincing.

When he chanced a glance at her, she was shaking her head. He even heard a tut, before she said, "You need to get out of your head, Cappelli, and spend some time in the real world with the rest of us."

And just like that, he'd lost his appetite. Around her, he'd become the one thing he strived every day not to be. Transparent. She saw everything. And he didn't like it.

When he didn't reply, she didn't seem too concerned. She continued on as if she'd not just exposed him.

"So … you said you had some more questions, about Marco?" A loaded fork was daintily pushed through those plump red lips as she eyed him expectantly.

Questions. Right. He had those.

Maybe think of them instead of staring at her lips?

Fuck. Clearing his throat and the filth in his head, the questions he had came flooding back to him.

"I guess I just wanted to know a bit more about his life. Was he happy?"

He was rewarded with another sunny smile. This one, slightly lopsided. "He was happy. We both were. We did what we loved. Traveled the world. Lived every day like it was our last. And as a good-looking guy, he certainly wasn't short of company either." She threw in a wink.

That was something at least. He had a good life. Marco deserved that.

"You said the other day you owe him everything, what did you mean?"

The playfulness drained just as quickly from her face as it had come. "Yeah, well, I also remember telling you that when I met Marco I was sleeping rough. It's no coincidence that changed after meeting your brother. For that, I'll always be thankful. That and everything else he did for me."

Luke's body didn't appreciate the reminder she'd been homeless, if the racing heartbeat was anything to go by.

"Like what?"

"Look, Luke"—her elbows hit the table then—"I told you, whatever you want to know about your brother, I'm happy to tell you. But I'm not here to share my life story."

That was bullshit.

"But your lives were interconnected, right?" he prodded.

She blew out a long breath. Clearly not impressed by his logic. Looks like he wasn't the only one hiding behind a wall. "Right. And I'm happy to tell you all about the places we went, his favorite food, the type of men he went for, or even his ridiculous morning grooming routine … but my shit is off-limits, all right?"

It wasn't all right. It only made him more curious. He wanted to take a bulldozer to that wall and uncover everything there was to know about this woman. But he couldn't. Wouldn't. So he settled for snippets.

He chose to hear more about the places she and Marco had traveled to. The adventures they had. And apparently the near misses to their lives along the way. With every story, Luke not only learned more about his brother, but Bella inadvertently revealed small parts of who she was too.

It was obvious that she had a fierce loyalty to Marco. What captivated him the most, though, was her sheer determination—and occasional fearlessness—when trying to understand why people behaved as they did. The places she'd been weren't exactly featured in any *Top Ten*

Destinations To Visit list, but when she talked about them, you would think they were. She embraced it all. The good, the bad, and the ugly, without so much as flinching. Where most people would pass judgement, she empathised. But the best part of hearing her talk had to be the way her entire face lit up, her body coming alive with excitement. So he asked to hear more. And then some more.

It wasn't until the wine bottle had been drained and their plates emptied that he realized how long they'd been talking. It must have been hours. But that wasn't the most shocking part, it was that his face actually ached from smiling so much and his throat was dry from laughing.

Did it make him a freak to admit that this had never happened before?

Yes. You're definitely a freak. A fucked one at that.

Maybe his first instinct was right. Maybe this was all just too much sexual tension for him to handle. Maybe if they slept together, he could move on. The knots in his stomach would unravel. And he'd finally be able to think straight around her.

There's only one way to find out.

As quickly as that idea came, it went. He was being dumb. Dangerously so. It was time to call it a night before he did something he'd regret. Gathering the plates, he hoped she'd get the hint.

"You walking out on me mid-conversation again, Cappelli?"

Bella stood then and began collecting what was left on the table. Glasses, the wine bottle, and that freaking candle, which he watched her blow out. The sight of plump red lips enough to stop him in his tracks.

Stop fucking perving.

With that reminder, his back snapped straight, and his previously gooey eyes became laser-focused. "I think I'll live not knowing what other weird thing you've eaten."

"What just happened?"

He averted his gaze again, ignoring her astute silver stare, and started to make his way back through the glass doors and toward the kitchen. "I don't know what you mean."

"Uh, yes, you do." He heard her scurry after him. "You went from normal and relaxed to cold and detached in the blink of an eye. Literally. Is it always that easy? Do you just flip a switch and the walls come back up automatically? No downtime necessary?"

Placing the plates in the sink, he swung back around to find a pissed-off-looking Bella in his face. Everything she was carrying a moment ago discarded, her hands were now placed firmly on her hips. A challenge sparkled in her eyes.

"Angel," he warned, not sure how long he was going to be able to keep himself on a leash while she was this close to him. And while the taste of berries was making his mouth water. "Has it ever occurred to you that maybe this is just who I am? *Cold* and *detached* as you put it?"

"That's bullshit and you know it," she spat. He found himself stepping closer as she spoke. Ushering her backward toward the floating marble island. "If that's who you are, then who was the guy I just had dinner with, huh? I want to talk to that guy. The Luke that's smart and funny and easy to talk to. Where did he go?"

As soon as her butt hit the counter, his hands went to the countertop on either side of her. Boxing her in. When his head dipped, his pulse pounded.

"Why can't I be both guys?"

He witnessed Bella's breathing pick up as he let his nose nuzzle hers.

"I think they call that schizophrenia." Her voice was a whisper. Her body betraying her words.

"What do *you* call it, angel?" Their mouths were so close now that his lips brushed hers with every word each of them uttered.

"Emotionally fucked."

Feeling his lips tilt up, he let his nose nudge hers again. "Aren't we all?"

"I can't argue with that."

He didn't want to argue with her at all. He wanted to do the exact opposite and worship her. Give in and allow himself a taste. Not just of those sweet lips but of all of her. Running his tongue along every dip and curve until he tasted heaven.

Just as the last of his control finally snapped, her palms came up and rested on his chest.

Fuck, her hands feel good on me.

Her forehead moved next and dropped against his.

"This isn't a good idea." Her voice wasn't just quiet this time, she sounded breathless. And damn if that wasn't as sexy as hell.

"Why not?"

"Because this can't go anywhere," she replied, stating the obvious.

"Why does it need to go anywhere?" he countered.

More hot breath sunk into his lips as she let out a sigh. "You don't understand ... I can't just hook up with my dead best friend's brother. It's not right."

"But if it were more than just hooking up?" He was playing with fire. He knew it.

"I don't know." He lost her eyes as they squeezed shut.

He couldn't give her more. What was he thinking asking her that? He needed to back off. Tell her he wasn't the "more" type of guy. But he didn't get a chance.

"It doesn't matter anyway," she said with a slight shake of her head, "'cause that's not gonna happen. That's not what this is."

Why did he feel like he'd just taken a punch? *That's not what this is.* Her words rattled around his overly heated brain. He wanted to protest. Demand she tell him exactly how she'd come to that conclusion. But that didn't make sense, did it? Not when it was on the tip of his tongue to tell her the exact same thing.

His brain and body must have spent way too long arguing with each other, because Bella was done waiting. She was pushing at his chest now. Releasing herself from the cage he'd created around her.

"I have to go." She avoided meeting his gaze as she rushed to get away from him.

He'd frozen. Everything inside of him wanted to go after her. But he stopped himself. Because what then? Was he seriously going to beg her to change her mind? No. Luke Cappelli did not beg. So he stood in his empty kitchen. And tried his best to swallow down the huge lump in his throat.

***

Luke needed some time. That's what he was telling himself anyway as he sulked on his couch.

Last night was still all too fresh in his mind. And don't even get him started on how his body was taking it. It had not forgotten either. It had been on high alert ever since his lips had lightly brushed Bella's. His heart was still hammering. His blood was still boiled. And his lungs were still filled with wild berries.

You're losing your mind. That's what this is. You've finally lost it.

It was the only explanation.

Vibration diverted his attention to the table. His phone was alerting him to a message. Slowly lifting from the leather cushions, he reached out and grabbed it, flicking open the message.

Benny: *Dude, you need to get your ass down to the Tipsy Cow.*

Luke: *What? Why?*

Benny: *That chick Bella is down here, and she's causing quite a stir.*

Luke had never moved so fast in his life. Within a second, he was up and grabbing his keys. A minute later, he was out the door. His brain hadn't even had the chance to catch up until he was in his car, driving to the Tipsy Cow.

What the fuck are you doing, dumbass?

It was a good question.

What if she's in trouble and she needs me?

Was this how all addicts justified their decisions, he wondered? Because that's what he was. An addict. He'd come to that conclusion one hour into watching ESPN. That's why his body was shaking, and he'd spent all day resisting the urge to go and see Bella. To get his fix. Now here he was, jumping at the first opportunity he was given to lay his eyes on her again.

Deep down he knew she wasn't in trouble. And if she was, Benny was there. He wouldn't let anything happen to her. But that didn't matter. Not now. Not while he was pulling up outside the only bar in town.

Car locked, pavement pounded, Luke was swinging open the heavy door just seconds later. Walking into the neon cave that was the Tipsy Cow. Colorful signs lit up the walls, casting pink, blue, and green shadows on the scuffed wooden tabletops.

He spotted Benny immediately propping up the bar. Luke's feet were on the move toward his friend as his eyes scanned the rest of the room. But he didn't make it to the bar. Or to his friend. His steps faltered around about the time he got his first look at Bella.

What the fuck?

In the middle of the dancefloor, the fallen angel herself was not only inspiring a whole load of sin in him, but half the damn bar too. She wasn't doing so in some sort of skimpy outfit either. She was in jeans and a flimsy vest. But the vest was rising up with every stretch of her arms. Exposing her flat stomach, her scar, and a black rose tattoo. The bare skin would have been enough to make him want to bite down on his fist, but the way she was swaying her hips in time to the dirty blues that was blasting out the speakers was enough to make him want to drop to his knees.

Apparently, he wasn't the only one who thought so too. She was surrounded. Men circled her like she was prey, eyes following every movement that sexy body was making. It was enough to make him see red. We're talking temporary insanity. That was the only excuse he had for what he did next.

Pushing his way through the crowd, he didn't stop until he reached her. She didn't notice him at first. Her eyes were closed, her arms were up, and her silky skin was still putting on a show. Altogether, it was enough to make him justify his rather caveman-like reaction as her eyes shot open.

"Luke—"

She didn't finish the sentence, because in one lightning quick move, he'd lifted her over his shoulder.

"What the hell?" He heard her shriek.

But he was too busy striding his ass out of there, nodding to a laughing Benny as he passed him. Just as they reached the exit, she began to kick. And then a punch landed on his back.

That's gonna leave a mark.

As soon as they were outside, he set her down next to the wall.

"What the fuck, Cappelli?" He deserved the push to his chest, so he took it like a man.

"I could ask you the same thing." Right now, his body was in charge, and it needed to be nearer. That's why he backed her up again, until she was pressed against the brick.

"What are you talking about?" Those silver eyes flashed in annoyance as he got closer. At least he thought it was annoyance.

"You can't hook up with me, so you go looking for it somewhere else, is that it? Is that why you're shaking your ass for the whole damn town?"

A hard slap stung his cheek. But it only made his blood pump faster, fire shooting through his veins and causing the thread he was hanging on by to finally snap. Next thing he knew, his head was down, and his mouth was crashing down onto hers. Fury fuelling every movement as his teeth pulled her apart. Prying her open to allow his tongue its first taste.

He felt her hands circle around his neck, forcing him down further so he could take the kiss even deeper. As he drank down every sexy sound she made, both of them fought for control. But he never had been very good at sharing. Which was why he needed to show her exactly who was in charge.

Both hands went to her ass, lifting her with ease as she folded her legs around him. Bella arched, and he pressed into her, her head pushed against the wall as he greedily took his fill. Satisfaction blooming in his chest when more whimpers vibrated down his throat.

He was so turned on he could barely think, all his brain cells long gone. Melted in the fire that was currently engulfing them both. Whiskey-flavored moans feeding the flames and threatening to burn them both to the ground.

If he wasn't in the damn parking lot, he'd have had her clothes torn off by now. His mouth all over this soft skin until her screams rang out in his ears.

But he was reminded of just where they were when the door next to them swung open, and the sounds of men stumbling out into the night managed to register in his cloudy mind. Their howls of laughter enough to cause Luke's feast to falter.

Shit.

Painfully aware of his predicament and what he must look like right now, he reluctantly drew back. Letting out a groan as he got his first look at her swollen, wet lips and the heavy breaths she was struggling to push through them.

"Come home with me," he panted. He was so far gone; he was even prepared to beg at this point.

"I-I." She didn't elaborate further. Just pinned him with dark gray pools.

"I'm not done with you, angel, not by a long shot." The scary truth was that he wasn't sure if he'd ever be done with her.

He didn't miss the heat flare in her eyes. "What does that mean?"

"It means that I'm not done making you moan."

His lips, missing hers already, went back for more. Lightly, he ran his tongue along the seam of her mouth, making her gasp. Now she was parted and ready, he scraped his teeth along her bottom lip and tugged—her taste dangerously close to making him lose his mind again.

"I haven't even started yet," he drawled into her. "You think this is good, just wait and see what else I can do with this mouth. I guaran-fucking-tee you won't be disappointed."

One night wouldn't be enough with this woman. He knew that. Accepted that. There was too much he wanted to do to her. With her. Over and over again. Too much he wanted to see. To taste. To touch. He wanted to drown in her. For days. Months. Fucking years.

Uh, years? What the hell?

Now was not the time to analyze. Now was the time for action. But she still hadn't answered. And his stomach was beginning to twist.

"Say you'll come home with me," he asked again, drawing back until he was looking into her.

She was going to bolt. He saw it coming almost in slow motion. Her gaze was no longer glazed. Her brain had obviously switched back on sooner than his. And her perfect white teeth had taken his place on her lower lip as she searched out his eyes.

"We can't," she began, wriggling enough in his hold that he knew what he had to do next. Let her go.

"We can," he argued as he set her back down on the ground. Not ready to step back from her just yet.

He was guessing the sigh wasn't a good sign. "I have to go."

As she went to leave, his hand shot out. "Please. Don't." Was he really going to beg?

Apparently, I am.

She twisted in his hold, a look of pure hopelessness marring her pretty features. "I have to. You *know* I have to. And you know exactly why you should let me. You're just as unprepared for this as I am."

"What does that mean?"

"It means, it's too much. *This* is too much, Luke." She gestured between them for emphasis. "I was wrong the other day when I said that anything between us would just be a hook-up. That kiss just proved that. And don't even think about telling me you didn't feel what I just felt."

He wasn't going to. She was right. So he dropped his hand … and let her leave. He didn't move though. He stood right there in the darkness. Trying to catch his breath.

CHAPTER SIX

Bella fidgeted in her chair. *Torture device more like.* She'd recently come to the conclusion that any chair that could be folded was not for her. Actually, they weren't for anyone past the age of thirty. She needed back support. Some cushions. Maybe a nice neck rest.

This is why I don't do activities.

Her job was adventurous enough. When she wasn't working, she wanted comfort. Peace and quiet. Maybe a nice book.

Not for the first time today, she cursed Luke. He was the reason she was surrounded by strangers right now. Pretending to fish. She hadn't even put any bait on her rod for God's sake. Not that anyone noticed. They were too busy snapping pictures for their Instagram.

Why was he the reason she agreed to go on a fishing trip? That damn kiss, that's why. Two days later, and her body was still buzzing. Who the hell kissed like that? Like he was worshipping her and punishing her at the same time. Setting everything inside of her ablaze. But the worst part was that she wanted more. So badly, she was even prepared to burn for it.

Fuckboys kiss like that.

Exactly. There's no way a man becomes that talented without a whole load of practice. But just the thought of that turned her stomach. Kept her awake. It didn't make any sense. Nothing about what she was feeling for the man she barely knew did. Which brought her back to why she was there. Joining in. Throwing herself into activities in the hope she'd quieten her mind, if only for a little while.

"So, you and Luke?"

Goddamnit.

Wade had snuck up on her. He'd even managed to drag his own foldable chair next to her without her noticing.

"There is no *me and Luke.*" Denial. Denial. Denial.

Wade scoffed. "Yeah right. He practically peed a circle around you a few days ago. And a little bird told me he made quite the scene at the Tipsy Cow the other night. You're the talk of the town."

Stupid small towns.

"Perfect," she grumbled, her eyes shooting back to the riverbed in front of her.

"So? What's going on with you guys?" Wade prompted.

He got her eyes again, but only so she could throw him a disappointed head shake. "*Wade Evans*, I never took you as a gossip."

A short, sharp laugh escaped as she got an eyeful of dimples. "Yeah, well, what can I say? I don't get out much."

Says the man always outside. But she was guessing he wasn't talking about the great outdoors.

"That makes two of us." She blew out a breath. "Marco, well, he was the social butterfly. If he didn't drag me out, I'd probably go months on end without basic interaction ... and be perfectly happy. I guess now he's gone ... I'm gonna have to drag myself out."

Her gaze returned to the ripples. A steady stream of green rapids glistening under the sun.

"It must be hard. Losing someone so close to you. I can't even imagine."

She nodded into the distance. "I miss him. Every day."

"Is Luke like him—Marco, I mean?"

"Complete opposites." She felt herself smile. "Marco

was full of life. He was one of those guys that everyone just wanted to be around, y'know? Always happy, always smiling. The eternal optimist in a world full of cynics. And Luke … well, granted I've only known him a week, but he's not exactly Mr. Sunshine."

She heard Wade snort next to her. "You can say that again." He paused for a moment. "You and Marco … did you guys ever … y'know… date?"

It was her turn to snort, after which she twisted to face him. "Marco was gay. So no, we didn't date. I wasn't exactly his type."

"Oh." She watched the wheels turn in Wade's head. "But I'm guessing you're Luke's type?"

Yet another sigh left her lips. "Does a man like Luke even have a type?"

"Wouldn't know, darlin', never seen him with a woman. He's not exactly the dating or relationship type."

Excellent. Red flags were slapping her in the face now. Mocking her. While she basked in humiliation.

Wade continued, "Doesn't mean he ain't interested in you though. If anything, you're the first woman I've ever seen him *openly* interested in. He's certainly never gone into a jealous rage before, thrown a woman over his shoulder, and carried her outta a bar."

She could feel the heat bloom on her cheeks. This town really did talk.

She had no idea what to say to that. It hadn't occurred to her at the time, but she supposed Luke's little display did scream jealousy to any onlooker. Despite what he thought, she hadn't gone there to hook up with anyone, she went there to dance. One of the things she missed most about Marco and her nights out. Dancing until sunrise.

Her silence clearly concerned Wade, because he was quick to speak again. "Sorry, darlin', I didn't mean to embarrass you." Yep. Her cheeks were bright red. It's official. "I guess what I was trying to say, not very well apparently, was that it's pretty obvious that Luke likes you.

And yeah, I get he's not exactly a 'light and sunny' kinda guy—from what Zach's told me, that's mostly down to having it kinda rough as a kid—but don't let the gruff exterior fool you ... I know for a fact the man is soft as shit inside."

"Yeah?" Her lips twitched at just the thought of Luke hearing someone call him "soft as shit."

"You ever see him around Libby or Cat or Rachel and you'll see."

Cat and Rachel? Why did the thought of Luke being soft around other women make her want to hurl so bad?

Hello, jealousy!

Wade must have seen her eyes turn green because he was grinning like he'd just caught her with her hand in the cookie jar.

"They're his friend's women," Wade finally put her out of her misery. "Cat is married to Cody; he grew up down the road from us and is our neighborhood cop. And Rachel is engaged to Hunter; he works at the fire station with Zach and Luke. Anyway, Luke might not admit it out loud or anything, but it's obvious he loves them and would do anything for them."

That was actually kind of sweet. It also wasn't hard to imagine him being protective of the people he cared about.

"Okay." She let out a weary breath.

She was done hiding. Wade was offering to lend an ear, so why not take him up on it? God knows she didn't have anyone else to talk to. Not anymore.

"Yes, something *might* have happened between me and Luke." She ignored the raised brow, and soldiered on, "We kissed ... and then I ran away."

"Why'd you run?"

"Because hooking up with my dead best friend's brother isn't a good look." She tried for a smile.

"Why'd you really run?"

Wade Evans clearly wasn't here for her bullshit responses. So she chose honesty.

"Because I felt something." Her head dropped at her confession, and she began fiddling with her fishing rod. "Something I have no business feeling for a man I've only known a few days."

"Do you think he felt it too?"

"Yep." She didn't hesitate. There was no way in hell he didn't. Fuckboy or not, you can't fake that kind of intensity.

When she looked back up, Wade had a thoughtful expression on his face. "So, what are you gonna do tomorrow, when you see him at the barbecue?"

That earned him a laugh. "I don't think you need to worry about that—there's no way he's gonna turn up. Not after what happened. Trust me."

"Hate to break it to you, darlin', but he's coming. He called me just yesterday to check what time it starts."

"He did?" She squeaked. Fairly sure she was now gaping at her host. And conveniently ignoring the heart palpitations.

"He did."

Oh shit.

***

Bella had a plan. She was going to turn up fashionably late to the barbecue. Grab a burger. Avoid Luke Cappelli. And then sneak off without anyone noticing. Simple. What could go wrong?

Currently an hour late, she had just rounded the main house to the backyard where the barbecue was being held.

So far so good.

She totally had this. And she actually believed that right until she got her first glimpse of Luke. Who had somehow already spotted her and was in the process of marching over.

Abort! Abort!

She couldn't just run. Could she?

She didn't run. Mostly because her legs weren't working. She'd frozen in place. Panic not the only thing rising as the

man she'd spent the past three days—since their kiss—
trying her hardest not to think about got closer. It was a
toss-up over what scared her more, the very real possibility
she might hurl or the look of pure determination on his face.

"Were you seriously gonna run?" he barked, still striding
toward her.

Wait, how did he know that?

"Uh, what?"

Good save.

"You were gonna run, weren't you?" he repeated as he
came to a stop, close enough for leathery peppery musk to
fill her lungs.

"No." *Liar.* "What are you even doing here, Luke?"

"I could ask you the same question, darlin'. You've
delivered your letter. Answered my questions. Made it *damn
clear* nothing is gonna happen between us. So … why are *you*
still here?"

That was a good question. Why was she still there?

Marco.

Feeling deflated, she let her shoulders sag. "Your
brother wanted me here, I don't know why, but he did. And
after all the shit he did for me, this is the very least I can do.
So here I am."

Luke took a step closer, his dark brown stare penetrating
her. "How long did he ask you to stay?" Was it just her
imagination or had his voice gotten deeper?

"A month." She found herself gulping.

"Good, 'cause we're not done."

She had a feeling he wasn't referring to the questions she
promised to answer about his brother, but she needed to
distract him. Or herself. Especially now that he was looking
at her like he was a minute away from swallowing her whole.

"We can still talk … about Marco. While I'm here. I
won't let what happened between us stop you from finding
out more about your brother. That wouldn't be right."

Another step and he bowed his head. Their faces just an
inch apart. Making it hard to think. "And you're all about

doing the right thing, aren't you, Bella?"

Was he going to kiss her? Surely not. There were people everywhere. His friends. Wade. Wade's family. The other guests.

As her rib cage began to rattle from the pounding, he let his forehead drop to hers and took a deep breath.

"You've got me all fucked up, angel, you know that? Not a day has gone by where I haven't thought about how goddamn good you feel pressed against me. Or the sexy sounds you make when my tongue is inside you. I need another taste. Just one more." His voice sounded just as tortured as she felt.

"Luke," she whispered into him. "People are watching."

"So let them watch," he rumbled, swooping down and capturing her lips.

Unlike their first kiss, this one was slow, controlled, and almost gentle. Luke's big hands cupped her face, tilting her every time he wanted more. Deeper. She knew she should stop. End this. But she couldn't. Didn't want to. Every sip of his lips felt like oxygen she needed to survive.

Her own hands curled around his waist. Getting her first feel of the wall of muscle that was Luke Cappelli's back and abdomen.

Holy shit.

Holy shit indeed. The man was pure sin. Made to tempt her. Whether he was frantically taking her up against a wall or giving her slow and sweet, no brain cell was going to survive his touch. Add in the deep rumble that was currently ripping through him and making her insides shake, and she might as well wave goodbye to all common sense right now.

When he drew back, she wanted to protest. Whine. Maybe even sob. What the hell was happening to her?

"Fuck"—his chest was heaving—"I can't control myself when I'm around you."

"Then don't." She gathered a handful of cotton and tugged him back down onto her.

This time there was no slow and sweet. There was only

urgency as their mouths parted and they both fought for the first taste. She felt a familiar tug in her belly as she wrapped her arms around his neck. Ushering him closer. Apparently, her body was done fighting her feelings. It wanted this man, and it wanted him now.

But her body would have to wait a little longer. They were both reminded just a minute later where they were, when a loud, so not real, cough broke them apart.

CHAPTER SEVEN

This was what happened when you didn't have a plan. You take one look at the angel you haven't been able to stop thinking about and all rational thought goes straight out the window. Any chance he had of resisting her was long gone.

Like you even had a chance to begin with.

That was true. There was no use denying she was the only reason he was there right now. At the Evans barbecue. He'd rather throw himself down a flight of stairs than socialize today. But he was starting to realize that for Bella, there was a whole hell of a lot he'd do.

The fake cough that had disturbed his second taste of heaven belonged to Rachel. She and his friend Hunter stood right across from them when Luke reluctantly pulled away and turned. Luke was hoping his scowl directed their way would do all the talking for him.

"Hey, sugar," Rachel chirped, "you gonna introduce us to your friend?"

Was she being serious right now? The look he threw her said as much.

When he didn't bother to reply, Bella was the one to speak next, elbowing him at the same time. "Um, hey, I'm Bella."

"Hi, Bella," Rachel beamed. "Nice to finally meet you. I'm Rachel, and this is my fiancé, Hunter."

Pleasantries exchanged, Rachel didn't stop there.

"So, Bella, the girls and I were wondering if you wanted to join us for drinks tomorrow night? We're hitting the Tipsy Cow in town."

That was when Luke snapped. He knew exactly what was going on. "No, Rach," he replied through gritted teeth. "She's *not* going for drinks with you."

The big man emitted a growl. Likely because he didn't say no to his woman, so he didn't like it when anyone else did either.

Luke watched as Rachel ran a hand up and down Hunter's arm, clearly in an attempt to soothe him.

"Uh, *actually*, Rachel, I think drinks sound like a great idea. I'd love to come," Bella piped.

"Excellent," his ex-friend chirped as she did a little bounce. "We're meeting down there at six—here, let me give you my number in case you need to get in touch with me."

Luke's eyes went to Hunter as the two women pulled out their phones. His friend simply shrugged. Where was the loyalty? Ten years he'd known his giant ass, been a good friend, and this was how he was repaid?

Feeling no less wound up as the couple said their goodbyes and went to rejoin the others, it was Bella who reaped the rewards of his bad mood.

"Why did you agree to go?" His head whipped back around to face her. "You know why she was inviting you, right? To get the gossip, find out what's going on between us."

"Well, she'll be shit out of luck, Luke, 'cause, quite honestly, I have no fucking clue!" She threw up her arms in frustration before pinning him with a look that in no way should turn him on. Yet it did. "Oh, and if you dare try and answer for me *ever* again, my knee and your balls are gonna get real familiar, really damn quickly."

Stepping into her space again, he took a deep berry-filled breath. "Noted."

"*Noted*," she mocked. "Oh, I get it, you've gone back to monosyllabic communication. Well, that's just fan-fucking-tastic."

He felt a smile break out. This woman was something else. Something he just couldn't get enough of.

"I'm picking you up tomorrow night," he announced, ignoring her glare.

"No, Cappelli, you're not."

"This isn't up for discussion."

"I agree, it's not. I'm a thirty-year-old woman, I don't need picking up after a night out."

"I never said you *needed* it," he clarified.

"Fine. Still doesn't change the fact that you're not doing it though." Her arms came up and crossed over her chest.

"These nights usually go on until closing, so I'll come by then."

Bella stomped her foot this time. "No, you will not, Cappelli. I mean it. You show up tomorrow, and you *will not* be getting a warm welcome."

"Because all of my welcomes so far have been warm and fuzzy?" His eyebrow lifted as his smile upgraded into a smirk.

He watched her huff through pursed lips, lips he needed one last taste of if he had any hope of getting some sleep tonight.

"You're impossible."

One more footstep and he was back where he was supposed to be. Her breath hitting his lips and his body close enough to encourage her crossed arms back down to her sides. "And you're fucking beautiful."

Her eyes flashed, and that's when he knew he had her. Neither of them could deny this connection. They easily generated enough electricity to power the whole damn town.

Taking advantage of her parted lips, he stole one last kiss. It wasn't sweet and slow or wild and urgent. This time it was claiming. His claim on her to be exact. He was done playing games. This was happening. *They* were happening. And he was no longer afraid of it. If Marco wanted her to stick around for a month, then that meant they had three more weeks together, and he wasn't going to waste a second more of them.

Letting his thumb caress her cheek, he drew back slowly. Memorizing every inch of a face that was so beautiful, it looked like Botticelli himself had carved it out.

"I'll see you tomorrow, angel." Even he could hear how rough his voice sounded. It was taking everything in him to walk away. But he had to.

Three weeks. He reminded himself as he turned. He had three weeks with her. And he was going to make them count.

***

As soon as he saw Hunter was on shift with him today, Luke knew that at some point he was going to get grilled. Apparently, that point was now.

Luke's first mistake was slumping into the ratty old couch in the communal lounge after a call out. His second was bringing a plate of chili with him to eat. And his final one was not getting the hell out of there when Hunter bounced down next to him.

"So, Bella?" Hunter began.

Fucks sake.

"Don't wanna talk about it, dude."

Hunter scoffed. "I bet you don't. Screwing your dead brother's girlfriend is a new low even for you."

Now Hunter was just pissing Luke off. "*Friend!*" Luke slammed his plate onto the coffee table in front of them, giving him room to twist to face Hunter. "His *friend*, asshole, *not* his girlfriend."

Hunter didn't react, just hummed. He forgot the man was the goddamn king of calm.

"And not that it's any of your business, but I'm not

screwing her," Luke went on, the words leaving a bad taste in his mouth. "She's teaching me about my brother, if you must know. Seeing as I never knew him, and she did."

"And that teaching includes sticking her tongue down your throat?"

He was totally doing this on purpose. To get a rise. "You know it doesn't. Say what you wanna say, man, and stop fucking around."

"Okay." Hunter kept his dark eyes on him. "You like this girl. That's obvious. But it has not escaped my attention, or anyone else's for that matter, that in all the time we've known you, you've never once brought anyone around. So, what's different about this woman? Why all of a sudden are you carrying her outta bars and laying claim to her in front of the whole town?"

Goddamn small ass towns.

He didn't have an answer. Not a good one anyway. Bella was different. She made him feel things he'd never felt before. Ache in places he didn't even know existed until she walked into his life. But he wasn't about to admit that to his friend.

Besides, this conversation was irrelevant anyway. No matter his feelings, whatever was happening between Bella and him had an end date. And if he was being honest with himself, that guaranteed end date was the only reason he was allowing himself the chance to explore his feelings for her.

"She's different, okay." He sighed. "But that doesn't mean I'm about to get down on one knee like the rest of you assholes. She's leaving in a few weeks, so whatever this is, it's already got an expiry date."

He didn't like the way his friend was looking at him. Assessing. Searching. What the hell was he looking for?

It was a good minute before Hunter spoke again. "You need to get out of your own way, man."

"Okay. Sure. I'll work on that." Luke was ready to tap out. But his friend wasn't done.

"This woman is the first to turn your head in thirty-five years, right?" Luke didn't answer. He knew it was a trap. "Okay, so I'll take that as a yes. Well, that means something. Stop pretending it doesn't. Do me a favor and just keep an open mind over the next few weeks, yeah?"

"An open mind?"

"Yeah. And whatever you do ... don't be one of those dumbasses who fucks up a good thing 'cause he can't pull his head outta his own ass."

And with that super unhelpful advice, Hunter was pushing up from the couch, his bulky six-foot-five frame swaggering back across the room.

Luke was still shaking his head as he picked up his plate. *Damn nosy ass friends.*

CHAPTER EIGHT

Girls' night at the Tipsy Cow was, surprisingly, a good time. Bella hadn't known what to expect, but she'd had a feeling there would at least be a few Luke questions. But so far, nothing. No interrogation.

The only time Luke had come up in conversation was when Rachel weirdly asked her if he called her anything unusual. When Bella had shared that on occasion he called her *angel*, Rachel had simply smiled. Other than a few exchanged looks between the women, that had been that. End of conversation. And Bella had to admit, she was relieved.

It had been a long time since she'd enjoyed a night out and even longer since she'd been surrounded by women. Nice ones at that. Libby, Cat, and Rachel were her brand of crazy. They were friendly, funny, and smart. And they also just so happened to like whiskey and dancing almost as much as her.

"Okay, ladies, I hope you're thirsty." A tray of shots clattered down on the table, a mischievous glint in Cat's bright blue eyes as she unloaded the tray and placed shot glasses in front of each of them. "Remember ... lick it, slam it, suck it."

Cat and Bella giggled while Rachel and Libby pushed at their friends' arms.

"If you start talking about you and Cody's sex life again, I'm leaving," Rachel declared.

Cat evidently had no filter. Combine that with her love of shocking the hell out of people, and you find out way more about a woman you only met three hours ago than you were expecting. Or prepared for.

"Oh please." Cat flicked her sleek black hair over one shoulder. "Like you and Hunter aren't going at it like rabbits twenty-four-seven. Besides, one of the perks of girls' night is when the guys have to come pick us up ... literally. Both of you would be lying if you said the whole 'caveman carrying you out of here' thing wasn't a huge turn-on."

Bella was saying nothing. It probably wasn't the best idea to mention that Luke had already carried her out of the Tipsy Cow once, and Cat was right, it was a huge turn-on.

She totally saw the smug smirks on Rachel and Libby's faces though. They loved it.

"Don't worry, Bella," Cat went on. "If you need to be carried outta here too, we've totally got you covered."

"Yeah, with Hunter being the resident Hulk, he'd totally be able to carry you and Rachel at the same time." Libby informed her while Rachel nodded enthusiastically.

"I think Luke mentioned he might pick me up." As soon as the words were out of her mouth, she regretted them. Especially when she got a look at the women's faces.

Damnit. Why did I say that?

Whiskey was making her lips loose.

"Really?" Rachel's eyes widened.

"Uh, yeah, I think so."

Too late for nonchalance now!

No one said anything after that. It was so quiet, Bella started to fidget on her stool. Just one look at their faces and she knew they were holding back, biting their lips and not saying what they wanted to say. Not asking what they wanted to ask. Of course Cat was the one who looked like she was in the most pain.

Bella rolled her eyes. "Okay, go on, you can say it. If only for Cat's health. She looks like she's one second away from exploding all over the place."

Surprisingly, Rachel was the one to crack first, grabbing hold of Bella's arm and shaking her as she spoke. "I'm sorry, sugar, it's just that we don't wanna scare you off with our excitement."

She was pretty damn excited all right. "And why exactly are you all so excited?"

"Because it's Luke," Cat said before downing her shot.

"He's never, like *ever*, introduced us or any of the guys to a woman. Let alone publicly shown any sort of affection for one," Libby added.

"And we're not just talking about that kiss he laid on you the other day." Rachel grinned. "I've never seen him look at anyone the way he looks at you."

"Let's not forget when he went full-on Neanderthal and carried her out of here too." Cat smirked. "Cody pulled that shit on me as well when I went on a date with Wade. He stormed into Casalingo, threw me over his shoulder, and stormed back out. It was kinda hot."

"You dated Wade?" Bella cocked her head in question. It was hard to imagine. Also, does everyone know about the bar thing?

"Nope." She popped her lips. "Didn't make it past the breadsticks portion of date number one."

Poor Wade.

"Anyway," Rachel brought them back to the topic at hand, "we can all tell he likes you, that's all. And now that we've had a chance to get to know you, we can all see why. Just don't hurt him, okay? He may come across as tough and like he doesn't give a shit about anyone or anything … but it's all an act. Deep down, he's a teddy bear."

Cat and Libby nodded in agreement while Bella found herself smiling. Luke really wasn't fooling anyone with the giant wall he'd erected around himself. Wade wasn't even friends with him, and he knew the man was, in his words, "soft as shit," and here these women were too, referring to him as a teddy bear.

"You don't have to worry about me hurting him. If anything, I think I'm the only one in danger of getting hurt." When she noticed the concern marring their faces, Bella was quick to explain. "Look, I'm not gonna sit here and pretend I don't like Luke. I do. But I've only known him a week, and as you guys seem to be all too aware … the man doesn't do relationships. So … whatever happens between us, it's not going to go anywhere. And I need to remember that. Maybe tattoo it on my face."

Only Cat seemed to enjoy Bella's sarcasm. The others looked like they'd just found out Santa Claus wasn't real.

"Okay, I think I need to dance now," Bella declared, downing her shot and pushing up from the tall wooden top table.

"Yes!" Cat concurred and followed her to the dance floor.

Bella couldn't take any more sad looks. She'd had enough sad to last her a lifetime. She needed to forget. That's what whiskey was for. And dancing. No more sad. No more pain. Just music and distant memories.

***

Bella felt Luke's presence before she'd even seen him. Like the last time she'd been on this very dance floor, she felt his eyes on her. Tonight was no different. When she finally decided to look up, her feelings were confirmed.

Luke was leaning against the bar. Big arms crossed. Giving her a look so intense that she was surprised she hadn't yet burst into flames.

Maybe drinking all night wasn't the best idea.

Granted, her control around this man when she was sober wasn't the greatest, but with half a bottle of whiskey in her system, what hope did she have?

Her first test came when those muscley arms uncrossed and he began stalking toward her. A massive gulp that followed didn't exactly fill her with confidence for what was to come. She needed a distraction. If only to get these damn heart palpitations under control.

As usual, he stepped into her space, dipped his head, and breathed her in, his brown eyes melting to black as he ran them down her dress. But she wasn't going to get lost in him this time. Not yet. She had an idea. Picking up one of his hands, she placed it on her waist. She then proceeded to do the same with his other hand. Once she was done, she dared a glance up. He looked no less wild.

"Dance with me?" She ignored the liquid heat filling her belly.

"Is that what you want, angel, just a dance?" His deep rumble was enough to cause a goosebump breakout along her arms.

That can't be good.

Letting her palms rest on his hard chest, she began to move her hips. They were going to dance. She was not going to flirt with him. And she definitely wasn't going to kiss him.

It only took one minute for her to realize that this was not a very good idea after all. Actually, it was a terrible idea.

Dumb, drunken brain.

Not only were they now touching, but they were so close that other body parts were too. Body parts that had no business being in close contact together. And with nowhere to look but into his dark eyes, back were the palpitations.

"If you keep looking at me like that, sweetheart, I'm not sure how much longer I'll be able to continue being a gentleman."

"This is you being a gentleman?" she teased.

"This is me not tearing that sexy as fuck dress off with my teeth, so yeah, like a said … gentleman." His eyes never left hers. He must have noticed her quiver. There was no chance she would be able to hide anything from him right now.

"You want to tear my dress off with your teeth?"

Shut up. Stop talking. What the hell are you saying?

A devilish smile graced his lips. "You like that idea, huh?"

She couldn't look at him anymore. Dropping her head, she chose to focus on their feet instead. It was the perfect time to remind herself of her plan. No flirting. No kissing. Platonic dancing only.

Yes, because all platonic dance partners tell you they want to tear your dress off with their teeth.

He wasn't having any of it. Lifting one hand, she found it under her chin a second later, one big knuckle nudging her up until she was facing him again.

"Don't hide from me, angel. *Never* hide from me." The vehemence in his voice only made her damn uncooperative body more excited. "You want me to stop talking, you tell me, okay? And I'll always stop. I swear. You need to know that I would never purposely do anything that would make you feel uncomfortable. Ever."

That's why he thinks I'm hiding?

"That's not … I'm not uncomfortable. That's not it."

"Then what is it?" She couldn't stand the look of uncertainty creasing his brow.

"I-I …" Her voice had gone quiet. "I like what you're saying to me."

His crooked smile stretched so wide she was worried for a moment it would hit his ears. "Yeah?"

She nodded. His ego had received enough words for today.

"Goddamnit, woman, if you weren't so full of whiskey right now, I'd show you that there was a whole hell of a lot more of where that came from."

Wait. Something clicked. She didn't have to worry about succumbing to his seduction tonight. A man like Luke would never take advantage of her inebriated state. He probably wouldn't even kiss her. Suddenly, she felt more relaxed.

"Take me home, Luke," she beamed, wrapping her hands around his neck and clinging on.

With a bend of his knees, she was airborne in no time, folding her legs around Luke's waist and drowning in deep brown.

***

When she asked Luke to take her home, what she meant was *her* home. The guest cabin at the Evans ranch. What she didn't mean was "Luke, take me back to your house and lay me in your bed," which was exactly where she woke up. Not that she protested last night. As a matter of fact, despite the haze and the slight pounding of her head, she was beginning to remember that she was the one who got into his bed. And possibly insisted he get into it too. There may have even been begging.

It was a memory that was only getting clearer and more horrifying as she groaned into the pillow.

Why would whiskey betray me like that?!

Thank God she was alone. She was embarrassed enough. The last thing she needed was Luke having a front-row seat to smudged eye makeup and bad breath.

Just the thought of what a hot mess she probably was, was enough to drag her face from the pillow. She immediately saw a note on the nightstand, next to a tall glass of water and what looked to be a pack of painkillers.

Congratulations, you really outdid yourself this time, Bella.

She tutted to herself as she reached for the note, not bothering to sit up. She needed the covers to hide her shame for just a little bit longer.

Went to grab us breakfast, angel, be back soon.

Shit. She needed to make herself human before he returned. Which could be any moment. The thought was enough to propel her out of bed and into his bathroom.

I wonder if Luke will mind if I use his shower. And his shower products. Maybe steal a T-shirt?

There was only one way to find out.

CHAPTER NINE

Luke had been the perfect gentleman. He was actually pretty damn proud of himself. As soon as they'd left the bar last night, all flirtatious banter had ceased, and his sole mission had been to make sure Bella had enough water to drink and got safely tucked into bed.

Yes, technically it had been his bed. But it wasn't his fault he wanted to keep an eye on her. What if she needed to hurl in the night? She could have choked on her own vomit. He was just being a responsible citizen.

Yeah, keep telling yourself that, man.

He also might have been in the bed with her. Again, not his fault. Bella had refused to let him leave and had even dragged him down onto the bed and insisted they snuggle. And whenever he tried to get up to leave, she whined so loud he was afraid she'd wake the neighbors. So he'd spent the whole night with her sexy body curled up in his chest. Breathing in wild berries and willing his hard-on down. Like a gentleman of course.

Now here he was, plating up muffins he'd picked up from Fairy Baked for her and getting ready to take them upstairs. All so Bella could enjoy breakfast in bed.

What has she turned you into, man?

The truth was, this past week, he hardly recognized himself. Not ever in his life had a woman had him so twisted. He'd never once wondered what a woman was doing or how she was feeling, and yet, now, that was all he could think about. *She* was all he could think about. And had been ever since the first day he'd met her, when she'd swayed that sexy ass of hers out of the fire station.

You're in way over your head.

He was. He was reminded of that a second later when Bella stepped foot in his kitchen. In his Woodvalley Fire Department shirt. Just his shirt.

Jesus Christ.

"Oh, hey." She bit down on her lower lip as her steps faltered.

Thankfully, he managed to push out the "hey" momentarily stuck in his throat. How could she look even better than last night? How was it possible? There wasn't an inch of makeup on her face, her hair was wet and sticking to her cheeks, and his shirt drowned her. And still, here he was, finding it hard to breathe.

"Are those muffins?" she broke the silence, her eyes darting to the plate in his hands.

Clearing his throat, he managed to draw in some much-needed air. "Uh, yeah. And coffee." The cup in his hand stretched out as he watched her hesitantly walk toward it.

As soon as she was close enough to accept the cup, he got his first whiff of his shower gel on her silky skin. She smelled like him. And for some insane reason, that turned him on more.

You're seriously messed up, man. That's some crazy shit right there.

"Thanks, uh, things are a little blurry from last night …" Shy eyes lifted to his. "Please tell me I didn't do anything to embarrass myself?"

His mind instantly flashed to his bed. Her head on his chest, his arm wrapped around her as she flung her own arm and leg over him. Did she remember that?

"No, angel, nothing embarrassing, I swear." Relief flooded her pretty face, and he was so entranced, he forgot what he was going to say. He forgot everything. His brain had stopped working.

Next thing he knew, the angel before him lifted up onto her tiptoes and lay a soft kiss on his cheek. Scrambling his senses even more. His brain had no chance of switching back on now.

"Thanks for looking after me last night, Luke." He was rewarded with a radiant smile. One he couldn't look away from.

Stop staring at her and say something.

He continued to stare. Still not talking.

Anything.

Nothing.

Come on, man, she's gonna think you're having a stroke.

"Are you okay?"

Yup. She thinks you're having a stroke.

"Luke?"

"Uh." His fake cough helped him stall. For a second. "Sorry, uh, yeah, I'm good. Shall we eat?"

He didn't wait for her to agree, he simply turned, grabbed his own coffee off the counter, and took himself and the muffins over to the kitchen table. He needed a minute to get himself together. He had a plan. A good one. And he needed to not fuck it up.

Bella followed him to the table, pulling up a chair opposite as she continued to eye him. Not hiding her confusion as she grabbed a muffin and began picking at it. This was not going well.

"You're being weird." She told him something he already knew.

"Yeah," he grunted. "I'm fully aware." He swiped a muffin too and wasted no time taking a big bite.

"Okay, are you gonna tell me the reason you're being weird, or do you want me to guess?"

He gave her his best "seriously?" look. Which she obviously took as a challenge and carried on speaking.

"Okay, um, let's see." Her fingers began tapping the

table as she pretended to ponder. "You … you think your house is haunted and you're waiting for the priest to show up?"

"What?" He might be smiling. Maybe.

"No. Okay." She nodded to herself. "Uh, you lost your lucky rabbit's foot?"

He just shook his head at that one. What was this chick on?

"Bitten by a snake?" she tried again.

He let his eyebrow raise this time.

"Weird itch?"

The table was treated to a spray of muffin that time. "Christ, woman, who's being weird now?"

"Well"—a mischievous grin started to spread—"if you tell me what's going on, then I won't have to guess, will I?"

If she really wanted to know, then so be it. The old Luke would have told her. What was he waiting for?

"Okay, fine. You want the truth? I'll tell you." His elbows hit the table as he leaned forward, his eyes holding Bella in place as his smile was replaced with something else. Something darker. "Right now, it's taking all of my self-control not to strip you of that shirt and bend you over this table." He heard her breath hitch, but it didn't deter him. His big mouth wasn't done. "See, Bella, I want you. I want everything. I want the taste of you on my tongue. I want to know how your soft skin feels pressed against me. I want to swallow those sexy moans you make while I'm inside of you. And see the look on your face as you come apart. I want it all."

Way to scare the shit out of her.

He still wasn't listening, and his mouth was still running.

"So yeah. I'm acting weird. Mostly 'cause I have no idea how I'm supposed to act around a woman I want so badly. 'Cause I've never been in this position before. And that's the God's honest truth."

By the time he was finished, he felt breathless. Despite their eyes never leaving each other, he was finding it hard to decipher her expression. He was starting to regret being so honest. There was a real possibility Bella was about to slap him in the face. Or throw hot coffee over him. Maybe hit him with a muffin too for good measure.

He would deserve it. A real-life angel was sat before him, and he'd just confessed every sinful thought he'd had about her.

Well, not every *thought.*

Luke lost her eyes as her chair scraped back over the tiles. He held his breath as she rounded the table and pushed him and his seat backward, making room for her. Her legs went either side of his and she lowered herself onto him. But he still didn't dare breathe. Not until her ass was in his lap and her palms were safely resting on his shoulders.

"You want me that bad, Cappelli?" Her head cocked to the side.

"Yes." He searched silver for answers.

"If we do this, then we need rules."

"What do you want?" That was better than what he really wanted to say. That he'd do anything she asked.

"I don't want to be treated like one of your hook-ups." A look of hurt flashed before she had a chance to hide it. It was enough to make him feel nauseous.

He wanted to be offended. Tell her that there was no way in hell he'd ever treat her like that. But reality set in real quick. He'd not given her reason to believe he'd treat her any other way. That was all he knew.

Until now.

"Never, angel." The words felt raw, like they were ripped from the deepest parts of him. "You could never be just a hook-up. That's not what this is. I know that. And I promise to do everything in my power to make sure you never feel like it is."

She gave him a single nod. "Look, I get that I'm leaving in a few weeks and whatever this is won't go beyond that … but I've never done casual. I've dated, I've had relationships, but being with someone, knowing it won't go further is new to me, okay?"

Why did those words feel like sharp stabs to the chest? He swallowed down bile and nodded. Urging her to continue.

"What I'm trying to say is … I need more than just jumping into bed."

He understood. At least he thought he did as he processed her words.

"You want to be wined and dined, angel?"

The look she gave him told him that, actually, not only did he not understand, but he was also very, very wrong.

"You really do only have one setting, don't you, Cappelli?" *What does that mean?* "No … I don't exchange sex for food. I'm talking about actual conversations, getting to know someone. To have good … y'know … I need to be able to connect with a person on another level. Something deeper."

"Oh." He did not know how to do that. "I've never … I'm not sure …" *Shit.* "I can try."

That was the right thing to say. Bella's head dipped, and he finally got another taste of heaven. A soft gentle glide of her lips over his, which was over too soon as she pulled back to get another look at him.

"Any other rules I should know about, sweetheart?"

A small smile graced those perfect lips. "Yeah. You have to promise not to fall in love with me, Cappelli."

Now that, he could do. Love was not something he was looking for. Or wanted. And he was pretty damn sure he wasn't even capable of it.

"I promise." It was his turn to capture her mouth now. He needed one more kiss before he began practicing the art of conversation.

***

Luke's gaze went back to Bella. This was not how he usually spent his days off. Or any day really.

When Bella had said she wanted to go back to the creek that ran through the Evans ranch, he'd obliged. Mostly because they needed to get out of the house. There were too many surfaces tempting him. Not to mention, going out meant she had to put on actual clothes. Something else that had been threatening his self-control.

The only thing keeping his resolve was his determination to prove to her that he wasn't a complete and utter dickhead. The look on her face when she asked him not to treat her like a hook-up was still burning a hole in his heart.

"You ready?" Bella asked as she bent to slide off her shoes.

"For what?"

"To take a dip?" She shot him a look insinuating his stupidity.

She'd lost her mind. He was in jeans. And she was still wearing last night's little black dress.

"No, clearly, I'm not. I didn't exactly bring my swimming trunks." He gestured down to his outfit as if to make his point.

She was laughing now. At him. "Wow, who knew you were such a square, Luke Cappelli?"

"A *square?* Seriously? What decade are you living in, sweetheart?"

Her giggles dissolved, and he was left with the sight of her blazing smile. He'd like to say, he kept his eyes on her face. But that would be a lie. Especially when she began pulling up her dress.

Sweet Jesus, Mary, and Joseph.

Black panties filled his vision. Immediately redirecting his blood flow. As the material lifted, he was treated to more smooth skin and that familiar rose tattoo. He was staring. Gawking really. And he knew it. But that didn't mean he could stop himself. A matching black bra was the next thing to make him throb.

God-fucking-damnit. How am I supposed to control myself now?

She knew what she was doing to him, that was made

clear as her dress was cast aside, and his gaze finally drifted back up to playful eyes.

"You coming?" She smirked.

Evidently.

He didn't answer. His mouth felt too dry. His silence was just met with a shrug as she gave him her back and walked toward the creek. That was about the time he had to stifle a groan. There was no back to her panties. She was wearing a freaking thong.

The universe was playing a joke on him. What the hell was he supposed to do now? Make small talk with a raging hard-on? Was that even possible?

"Fuck it." His shirt came off and hit the grass.

If you can't beat them, join them.

Next, his hands went to his buckle. Once he'd unzipped his jeans, they were unceremoniously pulled down. There was no hiding the bulge in his boxers, but that didn't matter, because he was a grown-ass man. And it's not like she wasn't aware of the effect she had on him.

"You pitching a tent in there, Cappelli?" she joked as her head bobbed above the water.

Why he was smiling, he didn't know, but he was. And it only grew bigger as he caught Bella's eyes roam over his chest while licking her lips.

"Trying to, angel. I could do with a hand though … if you're interested?" He sauntered toward her, cool water splashing against his bare feet.

"That line normally work?"

He wasn't going to tell her that he didn't usually need lines. That would only make him look more like an asshole. And that was the exact opposite of what he was trying to do.

"You tell me, sweetheart, it's my first time using it." That earned him a scoff.

As he submerged his body further into the water, he couldn't help but flinch. It might have been a hot summer's day, but this dip was far from refreshing. On the plus side, he probably wouldn't have to worry about his hard-on for much longer, not when his whole body was on the verge of shriveling up.

Musical giggles filled his ears as splashes were sent his way. "You really need to lighten up, Luke. You look like you're constipated."

Nice to know he still wasn't hiding his facial expressions in her company.

Taking the plunge, he dropped his body until only his head was above water. That was better at least. As he took in Bella, he started to unthaw. Sunlight was bouncing off her golden hair as it floated around her, while her arms waded through the ripples. But it was her innocent smile that had his stomach warming. She was so damn beautiful.

"So, how do we do this?" he asked as he floated closer.

"Do what?"

"This whole forming a connection thing? This is your domain, angel—you're the teacher and I'm the student here."

She took her time considering him. And he let her. Getting his own fill as she did.

She was the one to get closer this time, treading water until she was in his space. Her hands wrapping around his neck as he felt her legs go around his waist. When her body was safely curled around him, he found his hands going to the small of her back. To hold her in place.

Both of their breathing picked up. It was the only thing he could hear. That and his overactive thoughts. He was all too aware that in the short time he'd known this woman, he'd touched her more than he'd touched anyone in thirty-five years. He'd hugged her, carried her, held her all night long. And now he was enveloped in her. But that wasn't what was bothering him. It was the thought of not touching her. And in a few weeks' time, never touching her again.

"Having a connection isn't something you can teach." He watched her swallow hard as their eyes locked. "This is about getting to know each other, opening up and letting another person in."

"I don't know how to do that either," he rasped.

"I know." Her nose nudged his, and he took the opportunity to breathe her in. Even with the smell of his shampoo in her hair, he could swear he could still taste berries. "That ... I can help with."

Was he really going to do this? Let her in?

Three weeks. That's all, remember? How much could she possibly learn about you in three weeks?

"Okay." The words were scraped from his throat. There was no going back now. "What do you want to know?"

CHAPTER TEN

Bella had eased Luke into the whole "getting to know you" thing. She'd started with the basics—favorite color, movie, and music, and then she'd slowly graduated into talking about his job. What he liked about it. What he didn't. But as soon as she'd asked him why he'd become a firefighter, he shut down.

Baby steps.

Making out seemed to help though. No sooner had those walls gone up, than they toppled back down. And all it took was a kiss. Now that she knew that, it was going to be her secret weapon.

She'd need it. Especially when she ventured into the topic of his childhood. But they were a long way from that. He did continue to surprise her though. As soon as they'd settled onto the couch after dinner, he'd pulled her into his arms. And kept pulling until she was nestled into his side, her head resting on his chest.

It was where her head still lay. And she had to admit, she liked it. She'd never been much of a cuddler, not really. She was even starting to wonder if Luke Cappelli had managed to break her snuggling record in only a week.

No. Surely not? That would just be sad.

Sad or not, it was likely true. She wasn't exactly the poster child for healthy relationships. She also might have been slightly overexaggerating when she told Luke earlier that she had "relationships." Dating, sure, she did that. Relationships, not so much. Unless you counted dating and sex for a few months at a time, then Bella dumping their asses as soon as they started to want more.

"You okay, angel?" Luke's hand began gliding up and down her arm.

Damn, that feels good.

"Yeah, why?"

"You went all stiff in my arms, that's all. What were you thinking about?"

Uh, my shitshow of a love life.

Obviously, she didn't say that. "Nothing, it doesn't matter."

"Oh, I see. Is that how it's gonna be?"

She lifted her head to find him peering down at her, a smug smirk on his shadowed face. "How what's going to be?"

"You expecting me to open up ... but when it comes to you, it's optional."

He deserved an eye roll and a scoff for that, and that's what she gave him as she righted herself. Pushing against the leather next, she swiveled until she was facing him.

"That's not how it is and not really how it works either," she corrected. "For a start, you can't expect me to share every private thought. The same way, I don't expect you to share all of yours. And believe it or not, I am opening up to you, more than you realize. You're not the only one who's new to this, okay."

"Hold up"—Luke tilted his head—"what do you mean you're new to this? Is this the 'blind leading the blind' type of situation here? 'Cause if so, I'm confused. Weren't you the one who told me you needed this in order to have good sex?"

"Let me ask you something, Luke." She made sure her eyes were pinning him in place. "Have you ever gone to bed with someone you've actually spent time with? Someone you like, as a person … not just someone you wanted to fuck?"

She could have sworn she saw his jaw clench.

"I think you know I haven't," he ground out.

She did know that. But saying it out loud had the desired effect. "Okay, well, would it be so bad to find out what that's like? To know the person you're about to fuck. To *like* them. To care about how they feel. And to learn how they like to be touched. You don't think just those things would make sex better?"

Her heart was racing as she looked into a stare that was getting darker by the second. As soon as the words were out of her mouth, she began doubting them. Maybe this wasn't such a good idea. Maybe they should have done things Luke's way. One night. Get whatever this was out of their system, and move on.

It's too late.

It was. She knew it was. And so did he. That was made even clearer as Luke propelled himself forward, his big hands engulfing her face as he took her lips. She could taste the cocoa she'd made them on his tongue as she opened for him. But that wasn't all she could taste. No. He tasted like home. Felt like it.

You've finally lost it.

Maybe. Or maybe he just had her under some kind of lust-fuelled spell. It would explain the noises coming out of her as he lowered her back into the couch cushions. His big body fitting perfectly between her legs. It would definitely explain the brain fog too as he pressed into her.

He pulled back too soon; she needed more fog.

"You're right, angel." She kept her eyes shut as his lips brushed against hers. "I want to find out."

His heavy breaths mingled with hers. Then, all of a sudden, his hands were no longer on her face, they'd found their way down to her bare thighs. Pushing up his fire department shirt even higher than it had already ridden.

"Are we doing this … now?" she asked, her voice shaky.

Nerves were beginning to kick in.

His hands stopped at her question, everything stopped. "Open your eyes, angel." She was too scared to. "Please, sweetheart."

Something in his tone convinced her to try. When she did, she found him looking so deep into her, she could swear he saw everything.

"Not tonight," he simply stated, "tonight, I want to learn."

"Learn?"

"What you like." His stubbly skin scraped over her chin, heating her insides. "How you like to be touched."

That's what you wanted, right?

She wasn't so sure anymore. Not while her stomach was flipping and her body burned.

"But if you're not ready …" he went on, "then I'll stop. Just say the word." His dark gaze bore into her, searching her expression. Looking for answers.

The answer was clear then. Her body had overruled her head, not for the first time. She was going to let him learn. And in return, she would do the same.

With a nod, she let her nose brush his. "I want that—I want to learn too."

She didn't know if it was relief flooding his features, desire or longing, whatever it was though, it made her chest feel tight.

Am I having a heart attack?

No. Not a heart attack. Not yet anyway. But it was getting closer by the second as Luke's warm hands began caressing her thighs again, his mouth running down the length of her neck.

"I want to taste you, angel," he rumbled as the hem of her shirt hit her neckline, a growl erupting from the man who'd put it there.

No one had ever growled at her breasts before.

Is it weird that I like it?

This was not the time to question her sexual tastes, not

when Luke's mouth was covering her nipple and sucking so hard, she saw stars. It was safe to say she liked that too. But again, there was no time to think about that. Because her education was about to begin. It started when a hand pushed beneath her panties and a thumb circled her most sensitive spot. Her first lesson was clearly learning that Luke Cappelli could multitask. Amazingly, he could use his mouth and hands at the same time. Really fucking well.

As his teeth started to scrape, his fingers began to push. And just like that, her head fell back, and her body arched. "Fuck."

***

For the second morning in a row, Bella woke up in Luke's bed. But what was different about today was he was still there. His chest pressed into her back, a big arm curled around her and a heavy, hairy leg covering her thigh. She was surrounded by him. And it felt good. Too good.

After their little teaching session on the couch last night, Luke had carried her upstairs and laid her out on his bed. There might have been some more advanced modules being taught after that, but they still hadn't gone all the way.

All the way? What are you, a teenager?

That's exactly what she felt like. Fooling around had never been so good. It was safe to say that after last night, they both had learned what each other liked. And how they liked it. She should be happy. Ecstatic. She should be on cloud nine and shouting from rooftops just how many orgasms Luke Cappelli had dragged out of her. But as she stared at the trickle of light leaking through the silver blinds, only dread pooled in her stomach.

I'm in way over my head.

If she thought she liked Luke before they'd taken things to the next level, it was nothing compared to how she felt now. She was in deep. So deep, she couldn't think of a time she'd ever felt like this about anyone.

It's only been a week!

It had. And that made it so much worse. If this was how she was feeling now, then how much worse was it going to be in another three weeks, when she got in her Prius and drove away? Forever.

"Morning, angel," Luke rasped into her hair, his warm breath sinking into her neck.

"Morning." Her eyes fluttered shut. Just in time for Luke to dip his head and lay soft kisses over her bare shoulders.

As he hummed into her heated skin, his hand was next to wake up. Gently, he traced the curve of her waist, letting his fingers glide over her stomach and down toward her center. Getting so close, then drawing back. Over and over again. Teasing. Torturing. Until she was on the verge of begging.

"I think I need a refresher," Luke rumbled.

Her body instinctively arched into him. All too ready to obey. "Oh yeah? Scared there's gonna be a pop quiz?"

"I really fucking hope there's gonna be a pop quiz, sweetheart." Sharp teeth dragged over her shoulder blades, sending a shiver down her spine.

As screwed as she was, there was no turning back now. So she might as well enjoy it while it lasted, right? Twisting in Luke's hold, she turned to face him. Those sexy eyes were on her immediately, flames dancing in them as her hand dropped and she began stroking his side.

"You know where I hear is the best place to study?" she asked, just as his mouth tipped up into a smoldering smile.

"Where?"

"The shower." She let her teeth sink into her lower lip as she flashed him innocent eyes.

If possible, his grin grew bigger. "Then what are we waiting for, angel? I've got a pop quiz to study for."

In one lightning quick move, Luke rolled out of bed. Next thing she knew, she was airborne. Cradled against his chest as he strode toward the bathroom. That was when she started giggling.

"Who knew you were such a nerd, Cappelli?"

She was treated to a throaty chuckle as he set her down, his big arm stretching around her as he turned on the shower. "Sweetheart, I think you're forgetting what exactly is on the curriculum."

Bella took her time running her eyes over him. Admiring the very naked, chiseled view. She would have thought she'd feel self-conscious standing there, having also lost her clothes a long time ago, but after last night, it wasn't possible. Let's just say that Luke's tongue and her body had become very familiar. At this point, she was fairly certain that there wasn't an inch of her that he hadn't put his mouth on. Which explained the smile currently plastered across her face.

She watched on as Luke took a step under the cascading water and extended his hand. Accepting, she let him guide her inside the shower, feeling a familiar spike of her heart rate as he dipped his head and captured her mouth.

Splashes of water tickling her cheeks helped cool her heated skin as she tilted her head. She wanted more. She wanted deeper. And when she got it, she quickly turned tipsy as she inhaled all that he was.

Bringing her hands to his chest, her thumbs stroked muscle as she moaned into his mouth. In turn, she gulped down Luke's groans as he walked them backward, not stopping until her back was pressed against the tiles. When he snaked a hand between them, she felt that familiar throb. And ache.

Jesus Christ.

He was teasing her now. Just the way she liked it. So she let him. Breaking free of his kiss, her head fell back and rested against ceramic as she struggled to catch her breath. Once again proving that he was a star multitasker, his mouth came to her ear, nipping her lobe.

"If your plan is to try and ruin me for anyone else, angel, it's working." Hot breath traveled down her throat as he continued to nip and suck until she couldn't see straight.

"It's like you were made just for me. For me to *play with.*
Worship. Get so *fucking lost in,* that I don't ever want to be
found." His mouth clamped down on the spot where her
neck met her shoulder, and he sucked. Hard.

Her husky moan echoed around the porcelain chamber.
But he was only just getting started. She knew she was about
to get lost as one thick digit slipped inside of her. She could
only hope that she'd find her way back. Eventually.

CHAPTER ELEVEN

Luke was finding it hard to concentrate. When Bella was by his side, everything he was doing made sense. But when she wasn't, he was teetering on head-fuck territory. Which evidently meant he couldn't go a single minute without thinking about her.

After spending the entire weekend together, he was back at work, and missing the hell out of her. It was crazy. He'd known the woman five minutes. And yet, it wasn't just his body craving her anymore, it was all of him.

You're totally and completely screwed.

He was. He'd left Bella in his bed mere hours ago, and he was dying to message her. Find out if he could see her again tonight, after he got off work.

"Just do it," he mumbled to himself as he whipped out his phone.

Luke: *Up for another lesson later?*

He waited, staring at the open message like some kind of desperate fool, willing a reply to appear. The cushion next to him jostled, but he didn't look up from his phone. Not when he saw those three dots appear as she typed out her message.

"I never thought I'd see the day, man," Benny's voice filled the room. "You're so gone for this chick, you're *literally* staring at your phone, waiting for her to call."

There wasn't much to say to that. Luke was waiting by his phone, and he didn't care. So he decided a simple "fuck off" would do. And hopefully get rid of him.

It didn't. "So, I take it you guys are a thing now?"

Luke turned to look at his grinning friend. He was in no hurry to leave apparently. "Why do you care?"

Benny clutched his chest and gasped. "That hurts, man. I care!"

He turned back just in time to see a message from Bella appear.

Bella: *Sure, although, I'm not sure what else I can teach you. You're totally gonna ace the pop quiz ;)*

"What quiz?" Benny appeared over his shoulder. But even his friend's lack of boundaries couldn't wipe the smile off Luke's face.

An elbow in Benny's chest later, and the man dropped back onto the couch. "Oh, I didn't tell you? Must've been none of your damn business."

When Luke chanced a look at Benny, he was sniggering. "Look at you, dude, you're so damn happy, you can't even hide it. Who knew you had feelings and shit? You kept that a big fucking secret, didn't you?"

Luke simply sighed as he typed out another message.

Luke: *You can never study too much, angel. Pick you up at 8.30?*

"Oh, I get it, it's some kinky shit, right?" Benny wasn't done annoying Luke it would seem.

"Seriously?" Luke twisted to give Benny his full attention now.

"You're not exactly giving me much to go on here, man …" His friend shrugged. "Maybe if you answered a damn question every now and again, I wouldn't have to jump to conclusions."

Luke realized then that if word had already gotten out about Bella and him, then this was just the beginning. He expected to have to dodge some questions, but three weeks of this was going to end up bringing him out in hives.

"Look, Bella and I are seeing each other"——he watched

Benny go to say something, but he cut him off—"*temporarily*. She's in town for a couple more weeks and we're hanging out. That's it. End of story. When she leaves, I go back to being single again, okay?"

The grin was gone, and Benny's green eyes were narrowed on him. "So, let me get this straight—you're playing boyfriend with this chick for a few weeks while she's in town ... but after that, nothing, you go back to living your lives pretending that it never happened?"

Exactly. It was genius. Relationships weren't that scary when they had an end date.

"Yeah."

Luke was treated to a *tsk* and a headshake. "Another one bites the dust," Benny muttered.

"What?"

"I *said*, another one bites the dust," his friend repeated. "You really have no idea what's going on, do you?"

"What the hell are you talking about?"

Benny just laughed as he rose from his seat. A second later, he slapped Luke on the back. "I'll tell you what, we'll talk about it in a few weeks, yeah?"

He didn't wait for a reply, he walked away. Still laughing.

"Whatever," Luke grumbled as he went back to his phone.

A message from Bella was there waiting for him, confirming eight-thirty tonight worked. And just like that, back was his smile.

***

"Is that a mirror in your pocket? Because I can see *me* in your pants." Luke smirked.

Seeing Bella laugh-cry on his couch was the perfect start to his four days off. And all it took was him reciting cheesy pick-up lines.

"Are you from the Netherlands, 'cause Amster*damn*," he went on.

"Oh my God, stop." Bella pushed at his chest, giggle-hiccupping. "No more, my stomach hurts."

Capturing her wrist, he tugged until she fell into him and stole a quick kiss.

"See"—slowly pulling back, he was immersed in silver—"they totally work."

The goofy smile she flashed him managed to make his chest squeeze and not for the first time.

"I'm onto you, Cappelli. You may know some pretty funny pick-up lines, but that doesn't mean I've just magically forgotten why you felt the need to distract me with them."

Shit.

She was right. He might've been trying to distract her. Talking about his childhood was not something he wanted to do any time, let alone doing it after getting off his fourth twelve-hour shift in a row.

"Angel." He sighed. "I can't."

She took her time considering him, her expression turning serious as her fingertips gently skimmed his cheek.

"What about if you had an incentive?" she asked.

"An incentive?"

"Yeah." He didn't miss the devilish glint in her eyes. "What if for every one thing you tell me, a piece of my clothing comes off?"

Luke felt his eyebrows shoot up. Was she being serious? She wanted to play a fucked-up game of strip and share.

His eyes ran down her body. Shorts, a vest, and underwear. That was just four things. Disclosing four things wouldn't be so bad, would it?

Are you seriously considering this?

"Okay, angel ... get ready to get naked."

That was a yes then.

Her smile was back, this time scorching, heating his blood as she straddled his lap. "Real things though, Luke. Not the kind of bullshit answers you give to social services. You have to earn these clothes."

Real things. She had no idea just how *real* things were.

So tell her.

He went quiet, his mind trying to think of the last person he told his story to. But he came up blank. Luke didn't share. Not until now.

Clearing his throat, he decided to begin with the basics. The easy stuff that even a google search could drudge up.

"I guess Marco mentioned that I was in care, right?" He didn't wait for her to reply, he already knew Marco had. Besides, it was better to get this out fast. Rip the Band-Aid off and stick it back on quick before too much pus seeps out. "I went in just after my mom died—I must have just turned five. There wasn't anyone else to take me ..."

Like my dickwad dad.

"They say you don't remember shit at that age, but I do, I remember it all."

He stopped. Squeezing his eyes shut as he concentrated on the feel of Bella's fingers stroking his jaw.

"What do you remember?" she whispered.

His gut clenched. "I remember finding my mom passed out in the bathroom." He blew out a long breath. "I remember the needle in her arm." Another breath, this time his head dropped. "And I remember balling my fucking eyes out when I realized she wasn't coming back."

He was trying hard to push back the emotion threatening to spill out. This conversation was transactional, that was all. An exchange of information in return for a good time.

Yes, because a sob story is such a turn-on.

Apparently, it was for Bella. That was made clear when his eyes opened to the sight of dainty hands going to the hem of her vest and lifting. A darkening gaze pinning him in place as she shucked the material over her head and tossed it to the floor.

His hands automatically went to her waist. His thumbs brushing over bare skin. She was so goddamn beautiful. Beautiful enough to slowly unravel the newly formed knot that had taken up residence in the pit of his stomach.

"What happened after that … after you were taken?" Her head dipped this time, her hair falling forward and enveloping them.

He was back to focusing on the feel of Bella's smooth skin, quickening his caress of creamy flesh as he allowed himself to go back there. Back to the oppressive gray walls. The dingy, overcrowded bedroom. And the corner bunk where he'd curl up into a ball and count down the days until he was free.

"I was never adopted." Breaking eye contact, he instead let his eyes drag over her stomach. Then her waist, until finally they settled on where his hands still held her in place. "There were a few foster families, but things never worked out."

Because no one really wants to take in damaged goods. Not permanently anyway.

"When you hit a certain age, that's it. No one's interested in you anymore. So I spent most of my childhood in the group homes, and when I turned eighteen, I got the hell out of there."

Bella's hands cupped his face, drawing his stare back up until he was looking into silver again. But his eyes were betraying him. He could feel it. They were giving too much away. So he did the only thing he could do. He closed them. Squeezed them tight and pushed down the familiar ache that was already starting to clog his throat.

Man the fuck up, you've got an audience.

She gave him time. Placing two soft kisses on his closed eyelids. When he was finally ready to open his eyes again, misty pools were staring back at him. Into him. Seeing much more than he wanted. Enough to make him gulp. He didn't know what he expected to see. Pity maybe. Sympathy perhaps. Not the strange kind of silent acceptance she was offering him though, that was for sure. He hadn't even known that he wanted that either, not until she'd given it to him.

The seconds blurred together as they stared into each

other. He needed that too. Time to come back to himself. Time to soak her in.

It was Bella who moved first. Pushing off his lap and standing before him like a heavenly offering. He watched in awe as chipped red nail polish unbuttoned denim and slid down the zipper to her shorts. She studied his reaction, straight white teeth digging into her lower lip. This time he wasn't bothering to hide how he was feeling. The same way he didn't prevent the groan from ripping through him as the flimsy material was pushed down her long, tanned legs.

His vision was filled with lacy blue panties, panties that matched her lacy blue bra. He was well aware that the desperation he was feeling right now didn't make sense. He'd seen her naked plenty. Touched her. Held her. Made her scream. But this heavy feeling in his chest was getting stronger, and his fingers were only getting itchier.

"You're so fucking sexy," he croaked, not even recognizing his own voice.

A small smile tipped her lips as she dropped back down onto him. When she leaned into him this time, he was rewarded with a kiss. Slow and wet. Just how he liked it.

What has she done to you?

He'd worry about that later. Right now, he was opening for her, letting her take what she wanted and getting drunk on lusty whimpers.

Before long, his hands wanted in on the action too. Instinctively, they went to her ass and squeezed. Tonight was the night. He wanted her. Needed her. He was done learning. Done teasing. He needed to feel her from the inside.

When she drew back, he wanted to protest. He was only just getting started. And the sight of her didn't help. Add in the way she was looking at him—breathless, with pouted wet lips and heaving breasts spilling from lace. He deserved a medal for not tearing what little fabric was left on her and laying her out for his taking.

But when their gazes collided again, reality came

crashing back down. They weren't done. She wanted more. And he'd already promised to give it to her.

Fuck.

He could do this. All he had to do was dip his toe into the past two more times and then push the memories back down. Where they belonged.

Come on, man, you're an expert at this. You've spent your whole life shutting your feelings down, tonight doesn't have to be any different.

Yet it did feel different. It felt harder. Now that the box was open, it felt impossible to close. Could it be that Bella had broken him with all this "getting to know each other" crap? How was it possible to be in pain and turned on at the same time? Was this what relationships were like, he wondered? Was crying on each other's shoulders just foreplay for couples?

"Luke?" Bella's sweet voice brought him back to reality.

He simply nodded in reply; he knew what she wanted.

Just two more things. Two more things and then you're done. You never have to speak about anything ever again.

Luke knew he was lying to himself now. But if that's what it was going to take, then so be it. Ignoring the bad taste filling his mouth, he forced himself to push out more words. More confessions from a past he'd much rather forget.

"I never met my dad." His head dropped again. "He didn't want anything to do with me. Even when my mom …" He didn't finish the sentence; he didn't want to say it out loud again. "They told me he signed away his rights— apparently he even tried to get his name scrubbed off my birth certificate."

He was surprised just how much those words still stung. Even after all this time.

He looked up just in time to see Bella's eyes close this time. Sadness radiating off her in waves.

"Kiss me," he choked out. He needed to forget again. At least for a little while.

Her eyes flew open then. Hair dropping back into her

face as she leaned into him. He didn't wait for her. As soon as her lips got near enough, he scooped up and captured them. Prying her apart and angling his face to get deeper. He wanted to taste her. Inhale her. And not stop until he felt that high only she could give him.

It felt like the perfect time to claim his reward. His hands drifted up silky skin until they reached the clasp on her bra. All it took was one move and lace was falling through his fingers and luscious flesh was pressing against his shirt.

Now that there was something else to taste, he freed her lips and bent until a tight pink nipple teased his tongue. Nipping and sucking, just the way she liked it, he was rewarded with a throaty moan as Bella's head fell back.

Heaven.

This was something he could get used to. Unwrapping an angel every night of the week. Losing himself in her. Letting her help him forget. He was hooked. Again, his thoughts wandered back to relationships. Was this what they were all like? Was it always this good?

Feeling Bella slowly pull back, he sucked hard one last time before releasing her. They were both panting now with matching hooded eyes as their gazes intertwined.

"I'm done fucking around, angel. Tonight, I want you. All of you."

He'd given her what she wanted. He'd let her in. Shown her even more than he was planning to. He was done playing games.

She gifted him with a sultry smile. "If that's what you want, Luke ... then you know what you have to do. There's only one item of clothing left. If you want it, then you need to earn it." Her smile faltered then, replaced with a curious expression that flattened her soft lips. "Tell me what happened with Marco."

His body sobered in an instant. Marco.

Damnit.

He shouldn't be surprised. Marco was the reason she was here. It made sense she would want to try and understand what happened between them. But that logic didn't stop his body from reacting. Something inside him sank.

Come on. You can do this. One more confession.

And one more door open that he may never get closed. Was it worth it?

One look at Bella waiting patiently, and he knew it was.

"I found out about Marco when I was fifteen." Luke took a moment, averting his eyes as he took himself back. "He showed up at the home, claiming he was my brother, saying he was gonna take care of me. He was about to turn eighteen and said he was gonna get a job and an apartment and I should come live with him. All kinds of bullshit."

"What makes you think it was bullshit?" He felt Bella shift in his lap. He didn't need to look up to know what kind of expression she was giving him. It was going to be the one that liked to tell him he was wrong.

"One thing I learned growing up in the system is knowing when someone is talking shit to you. Telling you what you want to hear. Promising you things that they can't deliver. I heard that crap a lot. Why would his promises be any different from all the other people who'd let me down?"

"'Cause he was your brother?" She let the words hang in the air. He left them there. Absorbing the weight that label now carried.

It was only when she prompted him with his name that he spoke again. This time, he looked into her. Let her see him.

"To an angry fifteen-year-old, he was just another person who could hurt me." And he'd had enough of that to last a lifetime.

"So what did you do?"

"I told him to fuck off."

"And did he?" Bella's head tilted with the question.

"You knew Marco ... what do you think?"

A delicate smile gently curved her lips. She knew his brother was no quitter. As much as Luke wanted to reminisce with her, though, there wasn't a happy ending to this story and that smile wouldn't stand the test of time after what he had to say next.

"When he came back, must have been a month or so later, I was in a bad place. I was about to do something stupid … the kind of dumb shit you don't come back from. But he stopped me."

"But that's good, right?" His cheek received another stroke with her question.

"It is, angel. What wasn't so good was my reaction. I was pissed. Said some hurtful shit to him. Sent him away. And now …" He let out a sigh. "Now I can't help but wonder what if. What if I'd heard him out? Taken a chance. Let him be my goddamn brother … 'cause that's all he wanted, y'know? To be my brother. And I just pushed him away. Discarded him like day-old trash, when, really, I owe him everything. I wouldn't have the life I have now if it weren't for him."

Both of them fell quiet. Luke was done sharing, and Bella must have sensed it because she didn't push for more. Instead, she rose and stood before him, giving him a much-needed reminder of the reason behind his sharing session. The next thing he knew, she was pushing her panties down, and melancholy swiftly gave way to an overwhelming sense of pure want.

There was another feeling there too. Something that had been multiplying from the very moment this woman had come into his life. Something dangerous.

Bella clearly wasn't getting the same warning signs as him, though, not if her outstretched hand was anything to go by. An offer his body gladly accepted as he came to his feet and tugged her into him.

As her neck stretched back, astute eyes took him in, and all of a sudden, potential danger was the last thing on his mind. Which was probably why he let what was left of his mask drop. She'd been chipping away at it ever since he'd met her. And now it was gone. He was ready to show her who he really was. Damaged. Alone. And emotionally stunted. This was him. He was sick of hiding.

His newfound courage didn't stop his heart from hammering, though. Was this how it felt to let someone in? Vulnerable. Unsure. Fully clothed, and yet feeling just as naked as the beautiful woman in his arms.

"Take me upstairs, Luke." Bella's arms circled him. "I'm ready. Ready to feel all of you."

He'd never been nervous to take a woman to bed before, not until this very moment. Maybe because this felt more real than any other encounter he'd had. More honest.

As he took the sight of her in and felt her warm flesh press against him, he knew it didn't matter what he was feeling, because this was happening. Only an act of God would stop him now. He was taking his vulnerable ass upstairs, and he was going to feast on this heavenly body until sunrise.

Bending his knees, his hands went to her backside as he lifted her off the ground. Once she was secure in his arms, he headed toward the stairs, well aware that after tonight, things would never be the same.

And he was right. They wouldn't.

CHAPTER TWELVE

Bella stared at the ceiling. Her heart was racing. That couldn't be normal.

Maybe I should see a doctor?

How could things already be this messy? She'd known this man a hot minute. And here she was, falling. Like she was in some sort of romantic comedy or some shit.

Nope. Not happening. I refuse to let that happen.

"Morning, angel." Luke's scratchy voice wasn't helping. Nor was the feel of his fingers trailing up her stomach.

"Morning." She turned to face him, readjusting her head against the fluffy pillow. "You sleep well?"

"I slept perfect, angel." Reaching over, Luke laid a soft kiss on her lips. Only confusing her further. His forehead dropped to hers then, and she inhaled some more of the pure testosterone she'd spent the night drowning in. "Stay with me?"

That woke up some brain cells. "What?"

"Stay with me," he repeated. "Here, at my place. While you're in town."

Drawing back slowly, she dared to look into deep brown. "You want me to stay here ... until I go back to San Francisco?"

Duh!

Whatever. She needed clarification. "Yeah, sweetheart, I

do. I don't know if you've noticed, but you've been in my bed every night this week … and I like it. Plus, it's practical."

"Practical?"

What, are you a parrot now?

"Yeah, I mean, you won't need to keep going back and forth to pick up clothes and toiletries … you can just keep everything here."

Say no. You need boundaries. Like, you really, really need them. Especially after last night.

"Uh, I don't know," she rushed out. "I mean, my cabin is all paid for. And it's nice to chill out there while you're at work and …" *Think of something else. Quick!*

She had nothing else. She went quiet as she wracked her brain. No. Nothing.

"And?" Luke prompted.

She realized then that he wasn't hiding from her. His usual blank expression had been replaced by creases. Crinkles in his brow and wary lines framed his exposed brown eyes. His mask had dropped last night, but she had just assumed that it would come back with a vengeance the moment he wasn't trying to get laid. But she was wrong. And that scared her more.

"And … I don't know if it's such a good idea." She settled on the truth.

"Why's that?" He knew why. She saw it clear as day.

He just wants me to say it.

It was her turn to let her fingertips trail down his chest. She wanted to stay; she really did. There was no way in hell she had enough willpower to not spend every night in this bed. With him. And really, whether she stayed here or not, she was already in way over her head.

"You're not worried?" she asked.

"Oh, I'm worried." The air in the room started to become heavy as she held her breath. "But we're beyond that now, don't you think, angel? And it doesn't change the fact that you're still leaving in two weeks." *The man has a point.* "If this is all we have, shouldn't we make the most of it?"

Again with the points. Why did he have to go and make so much sense?

Leaning forward, she took his lips as her hand circled his torso. It was only when the taste of him was on her tongue that she felt like she could breathe again. Groaning into her mouth, he closed the minuscule gap between them by dragging her waist closer until she was squashed against hard muscle.

This man is dangerous.

But her body didn't care. Her body wanted him again. And it was painfully clear that her body was done listening to her brain. It was doing its own thing. With or without her blessing.

***

Bella huffed as she dragged Luke by the hand down the gravel path. He was being a child.

"Jesus, and I thought *I* was antisocial," she grumbled.

"It's not antisocial … *technically*, I do want to hang out with another person. *You*."

Bella rolled her eyes. Not this again. As much as she'd enjoyed the past few days, which had mostly been spent in Luke's bed, she was very much in need of a break. If she thought things were intense before, three days of mind-blowing sex really wasn't helping her to think straight. Or at all.

"Well, *technically*, you *are* hanging out with me."

This time, Luke tugged at her hand and pulled them to a stop. When she turned to see what was up, he was still pouting.

"Angel," he whined. "You know what I mean. This is my last day before I'm back at work, is it so wrong that I wanna spend it just with you?"

It wasn't. And she understood they were trying to make the most of the limited time they had together. But she was freaking the fuck out. She needed to be in a wide-open space and around other people who weren't constantly tempting her with their genetically superior body types. So Wade's offer to hang out today was perfect timing. For her. For Luke, anyone would have thought she was leading him to his death by firing squad.

"Honey." Her hand cupped his face, and she watched him soften. One of the many things she had learned about Luke was that when she called him *honey*, he was putty in her hands. And she wasn't above using it to her advantage. "It's just a few hours. We swim, we drink, we say our goodbyes. That's it. And then we go back to yours and get naked."

A smile split his pout in half. "Naked for the rest of the night?"

She started to chuckle; men really were simple creatures. "Sure, Luke, naked for the rest of the night."

He dipped down to lay a kiss on her lips. A kiss that was over too fast. But that was probably for the best, all things considered.

"Okay, come on, angel, let's get this over with."

It was Luke who was leading them along now, leaving the dirt path and walking straight into the grassy pasture toward the creek.

As they walked further into green, the hot sun sank into her skin and the familiar smell of freshly cut grass filled her insides. She needed this. She needed to re-enter the real world. Breathe in real air and not the leathery, peppery musk she was slowly becoming addicted to.

The closer they got to the creek, the louder voices became. She realized then that she had no idea who was coming today. Wade had been vague when he invited them. All she knew was that a few of them were going tubing and they were welcome to join.

Twisting to Luke, who looked like a man on a mission as he strode toward the voices, she decided to ask him if he knew.

"Do you know who's coming?"

He momentarily broke his rhythm to chuckle at her. "Why would I know who's coming, sweetheart? You're the one who dragged *me* here, remember?"

She nodded to herself, resisting the urge to bite down on her lip. "Just wondered if you heard from the guys, that's all."

A few minutes later, and it didn't matter, because she could see for herself who was there. Wade, his brothers, Matt; Jonah; and Zach, along with Libby, Cat, and a man who appeared to be Cat's husband, Cody. There was also a younger guy she didn't recognize, but Luke said his name was Benny, another firefighter.

After greetings were exchanged and a bottle of beer was shoved into her hand, Libby and Cat dragged her off to the huge picnic blanket they'd laid out.

"Where's Rachel?" Bella asked.

"Oh"—Libby giggled—"she and Hunter couldn't make it."

"They're banging," Cat announced, pulling a giggle out of Bella too. Good to know.

Not unlike their girls' night, dirty jokes were next to be made. Then, the questions started. Questions Bella knew were coming. You didn't get to play a temporary couple without people asking questions.

"So, you guys are a thing now … officially?" Libby nodded toward Luke, who stood around in a circle with the other men.

Her eyes went to and stayed on Luke as she answered, "Yeah, I guess we are. Until I leave."

"And after that?" Cat asked.

She let a sigh slip, her gaze going back to the two women sitting cross-legged in front of her. "After that, I go home. And we both go back to our lives."

"And you're cool with that?" Libby didn't seem very enthused.

Bella's eyes dropped to her own crossed legs. "I don't think I have a choice."

"So that's it?" Libby wasn't doing a great job at hiding her frustration. "You both like each other, but you're not even gonna try? That's just dumb. Can't you do long distance for a while? Where do you live again?"

"Uh, San Francisco"—Bella began to fidget—"but I guess I'm kinda between places right now. Marco and I had an apartment together, but after … Well, it was too big for just me, so I didn't renew the lease. My stuff is all in storage, so when I head back, I'll need to start looking for a place."

"Oh my God," Libby squealed, "that means you could move here, to Woodvalley. You wouldn't even have to do much, 'cause your apartment's all packed up!"

"Um, what?" Bella was pretty sure her face was contorting just as fast as her heart was beating. "No, that's not what … I don't think. Um, no. Just, no."

"Way to scare the shit outta her, Lib." Cat smirked as she reached over to the cooler and pulled out a beer.

Bella didn't even deny it. The woman was scaring her. There was no way in hell she would be moving to Woodvalley. Talk about total bunny boiler behavior. The last thing she needed was Luke taking out a restraining order on her ass.

"Sorry, I just meant that you travel for work, right?" Libby didn't wait for Bella to confirm before continuing, "Well, I got the impression you're not home a lot because of your job, and I remember you saying Marco was your only friend … and you didn't mention any family—so I just assumed there wasn't much keeping you there. If that's the case, then why not move?"

Wow. No friends. No family. Reality slapping you in the face really stings that much more when it's coming out of someone else's mouth.

"What Lib is trying to say," Cat jumped in, "is that you have friends here now. Me, Lib, and Rach. And if there's nothing waiting for you back home, *we'd* like you to stick around … whatever happens with you and Luke."

A wave of emotions washed over Bella as warmth

blossomed in her chest. Why were these women being so nice to her? People were never really that nice to her. She hadn't even ever had a close girlfriend before. And now suddenly she had three. It didn't make sense.

"But you guys hardly know me?" she let slip.

Matching smiles were pasted on Cat and Libby's faces.

Libby was the first to speak. "Is it that hard to believe that we like you?"

Yes. "I've not had any female friends before." *Seriously? Where the hell is my "Don't sound like a loser" filter?*

"Well, now you do," Cat replied before taking a swig of her beer.

Bella felt her lips tip just as Wade called out for everyone to make their way over to the creek.

It was time to tube.

***

"Why were you living on the street?"

Of all the times to have this conversation, Bella wasn't expecting it to be now. In a fancy Italian restaurant. Her mouth full of pasta. Pasta she still had to finish chewing while Luke's eyes pinned her in place.

She knew this question was coming. He'd opened up to her last week, and now it was her turn. But Luke was well aware that she didn't want to talk about it. Maybe that's why he'd suggested taking her out for dinner after his shift tonight and plied her with her favorite food. To soften the blow.

Taking her time to swallow down her penne and then following up with a long, slow sip of wine, his gaze didn't waver. And his paused fork meant his bolognese was paying the price for her stalling and getting colder by the second.

"I told you," she finally caved. "I'm no stranger to dysfunctional families."

"That's not an answer." A condescending *tsk* came just moments later.

"Says who?"

"Says me." His facial features may have been set to serious, but she totally noticed a lip twitch.

One dramatic sigh later, her fork was reluctantly placed on her plate. "Look, it's a long story, okay? And I'm not sure right now"—her eyes scanned the candlelit restaurant before returning to him—"is the time to talk about it."

"I beg to differ."

"Of course you do."

She was gifted with another twitch of the lips before he spoke again. "Do you need an incentive, angel?"

It was her turn to curl her lips, this one made it all the way into a mischievous grin. "You planning on putting on a strip show in the middle of Casalingo, Luke?" Not that she'd be opposed to it.

"No, sweetheart, I was thinking more of a share-for-share deal." He leaned forward, his arms resting on the white tablecloth. "You share, I share. Answer a question, you get to ask me one … and vice versa."

So much for a light and chilled night. Things were about to get real depressing. But she knew she needed to give him something, especially after what he'd given her. The truth was, since they'd slept together, the fortress Luke had built around himself had crumbled. He wasn't hiding. Or dodging questions. He was opening up, freely. Sharing stories from his childhood, ranging from his time in care to his favorite foster family, the Coulthards. No prompting necessary. And it was beautiful to witness.

So stop hiding from him.

Easier said than done. But seeing as one crack in the foundation wouldn't bring down an entire wall, she decided to give it a try. After a little more liquid courage. She gave him a nod as she drained the last of her drink.

"My parents were addicts." Another sigh left her lips. "Meth, in case you were wondering." Luke purposely wasn't reacting; his serious expression was firmly in place and all amusement that had been there a second ago was gone. "My childhood was pretty rough, I guess. I'm not gonna bore you with the details, but let's just say it eventually ended in us losing our trailer ... hence the homelessness."

"How old were you?" Okay, now he looked pissed off. And sounded like it too. What was she supposed to do with that?

Ignore it?

"Fifteen."

"Fifth-fucking-teen?" he seethed. "And your parents? Were they right there beside you on the street?"

Bella shifted in her seat. If he was angry at that, it didn't bode well for the rest of the story.

She shook her head before replying, preparing him for what was to come. "I don't know where they were. They just left. Which wasn't that unusual. I was used to them being gone for days at a time—sometimes even weeks. I was used to looking after myself, you know? And, really, it wasn't so bad, you just had to scout out the best spots and find good restrooms to wash up in ... it could have been a lot worse ... I wasn't even doing it for that long, not really, not compared to other people and ..." She trailed off as soon as she caught sight of Luke's face.

Wow, he's really red.

"Are you okay?" It was a pointless question. She asked it anyway.

"No, Bella, I'm not okay. How can you sit there and say with a straight face that living on the streets, by yourself, at fifteen ... *wasn't so bad?* Do you really believe that, or are you just telling me what I want to hear?"

Am I telling him what he wants to hear? Shit. Maybe I am. Why would I do that?

He was right. It was bad. Even if it was only for a few months, it still managed to fuel a lifetime of nightmares.

"It was horrible, okay," she rushed out. "Is that what you want to hear? I was scared shitless. All the time. There wasn't a second that went by where I wasn't terrified for my life or what might happen to me once the sun went down.

There. I said it. But sitting here repeating some sob story doesn't change anything, Luke. It doesn't make it better. Or hurt any less. It's just a reminder of my shit family. A reminder, to be quite honest with you, I don't *want* or *need*."

The next thing she knew, Luke was out of his chair and pulling out hers. Taking her hand, he tugged her to her feet and wrapped his big arms around her. Until she was surrounded by him. Breathing in leather and absorbing the comfort of his steady heartbeat as she nestled her head into the crook of his neck.

"I'm sorry, angel," he whispered into her hair. "I wish I could take it away. Make it better. Make it so it never happened."

"But then I wouldn't be me," she mumbled into his crisp cotton shirt.

She felt him let out a heavy breath as his grip on her tightened. "No, sweetheart, you wouldn't."

"And if you didn't have such a shitty childhood, you wouldn't be *you* either," she added.

She wouldn't change one thing about him. Every sharp edge, every jagged tear, and every brick he'd surrounded his heart with, made him the man he was today. An amazing man. A real-life, firefighting hero. Who was kind. And loving. And really fucking bad at hiding the softness lurking beneath the darkness.

"Maybe that wouldn't be such a bad thing." He sighed into her.

"Bullshit." She pulled back just enough to look into his eyes. "You think I don't see you, Luke Cappelli? You think I don't know how incredible you are? How strong? How much you give a shit? I see you. I—"

She didn't get to finish. She was cut off by Luke's mouth crashing down onto hers and pushing her lips open. Tasting her with enough urgency, even the spices on his tongue managed to fry a few brain cells as her body set alight.

If people weren't already looking, she had no doubt, they were now. Luke and she were putting on a show. But that was the last thing on her mind as her hand curled around his thick neck, dragging him closer. Trying to get deeper. Begging his mouth to take away the ache.

She drank down every groan he made as if it would satisfy her thirst. It didn't.

"Uh," a voice next to them started to register in her fuzzy brain, but she didn't stop. She indulged in another taste. "Uh, Luke?"

Luke finally released her, drawing back slowly, his eyes not leaving hers even as he addressed the man beside them. The voice she now recognized as the waiter's.

"I think we're gonna need the check, Nico. Can you box up the rest of our food and throw in two tiramisus to go while you're at it?"

A huge grin was pasted on her face, so big, she was surprised her jaw didn't ache.

Behold, the perfect man.

Pasta. Tiramisu. And Luke naked. It was going to be a good night after all.

CHAPTER THIRTEEN

Luke couldn't decide on whether he needed a doctor or a smack in the face.

A smack would be cheaper.

Last night, in the middle of Casalingo, he felt it. Something he'd never felt before, yet he knew exactly what it was. And it was something that definitely wasn't going away anytime soon. Even if Bella was.

Just the thought of how he was going to feel when she walked away had him shaking his head as he locked his car and started toward the apartment complex.

Goddamn.

He wasn't equipped for this. Opening up to someone had clearly dislodged something in his brain. Broken it. Broken him.

As if I wasn't already fucked up enough.

He didn't have time to dwell on that now though. One shitshow at a time. Today's trauma took precedent.

Using his spare key, he decided not to buzz up and went straight inside the building. Climbing the stairs two at a time until he reached the second floor.

After ringing the bell, he chuckled to himself as he heard feminine curses getting louder and louder through the wood. Before long, he was treated to the sight of a dishevelled-looking Rachel.

"Luke! What are you doing here?"

"Bad time?" His lips quirked.

Not phased in the slightest, Rachel tucked a strand of long red hair behind her ear as a warm smile spread across her face. "Nah, not for you, sugar. Come on in."

The door widened and he stepped through, following Rachel into the living room. His eyes scanned the surroundings as he took a seat on the L-shaped gray couch. Hunter's previously muted décor had been replaced with diamanté-covered frames, a huge pink statement wall behind the flatscreen, and his once-empty shelves were teaming with new useless knickknacks.

"Jesus Christ, woman, what the hell have you done to this place?"

Rachel beamed his way as she bounced down next to him. "Did you come here just to critique my decorating skills, or was there an actual reason?"

That's one of the things he liked about Rachel. He could tease her like one of the guys and she couldn't care less. It made it easier to be himself around her. Maybe that's why they'd gotten so close over the past few months. That and Hunter getting shot, of course.

"Actually, I came here for some advice."

"If it's about Bella, I love her, and yes, you should ask her to marry you and have lots of babies."

Not even throwing her his dirtiest look was enough to do that ridiculous statement justice. He threw it anyway.

"Fucking hell, woman." His hand went through his mop of hair as he continued to shake his head. "No. Just no. It's not about Bella, it's about my dad, okay."

Not hiding her surprise, Rachel twisted on the sofa, giving him her full attention. "Okay?"

"Your dad didn't want you, right?"

"Gee, Luke, you seriously need to work on your people skills." When he didn't reply, she carried on, "Actually, it was my mom who didn't want me. My dad was just shit."

He nodded, his gaze dropping to his lap momentarily

before he met Rachel's curious blue eyes again as she studied him.

"My dad didn't want me," he croaked. "All my life, I just assumed it was 'cause I was a mistake. That he was never really with my mom, and he didn't wanna step up after he got her pregnant." He went silent as Rachel shifted closer, understanding clear on her face. Pushing through the brand-new crack in his voice, he continued, "But then Bella turns up with this letter from Marco. A man I thought was my half brother. Another kid my dad didn't wanna take responsibility for. And now I don't know what to think."

"What did it say? The letter, I mean."

"A whole hell of a lot. The most fucked up thing being that Marco wasn't my half brother after all … his mom was actually my mom, which makes him my *full* brother, I guess."

"What?" Rachel gasped. "How? Why didn't anyone tell you? What does that mean?"

"Exactly." Luke slumped back into the cushions. "How the fuck did I not know that? And what am I supposed to do with that information now? It's too late. He's gone. It's not like we're gonna be able to bond. And it brings up a whole host of other shit and guilt and unanswered questions."

"Like?"

He could feel Rachel's eyes on him, but his gaze was ahead. Not wavering from the flatscreen.

"Like … I feel guilty for not trying earlier. He came to see me when I was a kid, and I brushed him off. Thinking he was just one of many half-siblings my dad had abandoned. And then there's the fact that my mom was with my dad. Like in an actual relationship. That's pretty damn hard to swallow. It means not only did he leave me, but he left her too."

"Wait … if Marco was older than you, why didn't you grow up together until your mom …?"

"Died?" He finished the sentence for her. "He said in

the letter social services removed him. Took away their custody." His mom was an addict, so Luke assumed that was why Marco had been taken away. Which made sense. What didn't make sense was why they hadn't taken him too. Before she'd overdosed.

Rachel let out a few choice curse words next to him before slumping back into the cushions, mirroring his position and staring ahead at the blank screen. They were both quiet after that. It was a good few minutes before his friend finally broke the silence.

"When Marco came to see you, when you were a kid, what happened?"

Luke's eyes squeezed shut. He could still see the look on his brother's face. The disappointment.

"The first time, I didn't exactly give him a warm welcome. And the second time ..." Luke let out a heavy breath. "The second time ... he turned up at the group home and caught me doing something I shouldn't have been doing."

"What does that mean?" He didn't need to see to know that Rachel's eyes were boring into him.

"It means I was an angry fifteen-year-old, sick of living in group homes, and I wanted out. And I stupidly thought stealing from the cash box and jacking the manager's car would be enough to set me up."

He was an idiot. It was the dumbest thing he'd ever done. Something he still regretted to this very day.

"So ... not a great first impression, huh?"

He could hear the amusement in Rachel's voice. It was enough for him to open his eyes and turn his head toward her. Yes. He was right. Big ass smile.

"You think that's funny, huh?"

"I mean, it's a little funny. You obviously think that makes you the worst person in the world or you wouldn't be acting so dramatic."

"Rach, I could have gone to jail ... gotten a record. It could have stopped me from becoming a firefighter." How was she not getting this?

Her whole body twisted until the side of her cheek was pressed up against the gray cotton cushion. "You were just a kid. Besides, I take it your brother stopped you. Talked some sense into you?"

"Yeah. He did. 'Cause I'm the screw-up and he's the literal award winner in this fucked-up family." His hand ran over the top of his shaking head. "I couldn't even be nice to him. He wanted to help me. *Know* me. But I told him to leave. Told him I wanted nothing to do with him."

That feeling in his stomach that had been there ever since he'd read Marco's letter was bubbling again. Enough to cause acid to rise up until the taste of guilt bathed his tongue. What would have happened if he hadn't chased his brother away that day? How would his life have turned out? He would have had a family. A brother. Someone to spend holidays with. Someone to rely on. Someone to call when things went bad.

I wouldn't be alone.

"Stop!" Rachel cried, snapping him out of his melancholic musings. "You need to stop, sugar. You're beating yourself up over something that happened twenty years ago."

"I was an asshole."

"So what's new?" Rachel's hand went to his arm, tugging until she'd managed to twist his body to face her. "Seriously, Luke, you were *fifteen*. Cut yourself some slack. Besides, what was stopping Marco from trying again anyway? He knew where you were, clearly. And he never forgot you … otherwise he wouldn't have written that crazy letter. Stop putting all this on you."

"I should have reached out. I should have given a shit."

"Yeah, and I shoulda bought that winning lottery ticket last week too," Rachel mocked. "Sugar, the past is the past. If you're living in it, then you're doing something wrong. You came here for advice, right?"

Luke grunted.

"Well, my advice is to snap out of it." She had got to be kidding. He gave her a look that conveyed as much too. Which she ignored. "You're not the only one who would love to go back and change something they did in the past, and you won't be the last. But seeing as that's not gonna happen, you need to work with what you've got now. You may not have had a chance to get to know your brother when he was alive, but you've been given a rare chance to get to know him now. Through Bella. Don't waste that. Don't let this opportunity be another one you'll regret not taking."

It killed him to admit it, but Rachel was right. He couldn't change the past. He had no other choice but to live with it. That and his new stomachache.

Another grunt and Rachel was pulling him into a hug. Rachel hugging him wasn't new. The lack of awkwardness, though, was. He actually didn't mind it.

That's a first.

Was it though? It was no coincidence that he'd spent the past couple of weeks curled up with Bella. Maybe all that physical contact had done something to him. Another part of him was broken.

Or fixed.

"Okay." He sighed as he pulled back from her embrace. "I'm ready to talk about Bella now."

"Yeah?" Rachel grinned.

"Yeah."

Here goes nothing.

***

"Hey?" Bella's head left his chest, and he got his first look at the concern in her eyes. "You okay?"

"Yeah, angel, I'm good."

"You sure? You went pretty quiet." Bella tipped her head to the side until messy blonde hair brushed her cheek.

"I was just thinking about Marco. Do you think …?"

Luke paused, giving him a chance to swallow down any hesitancy he had. "Do you think we could watch some of his documentaries together?"

He was rewarded with that big beautiful smile he'd grown accustomed to. "Of course. I have them all on my laptop. We can hook it up to your TV and watch them whenever you want."

"Wanna watch one now?"

Bella jumped up from the couch and was out of his arms before he had a chance to blink. He already knew where she was headed. The kitchen. He'd seen her laptop in there earlier. She'd taken to working in there most days.

Despite her initial protests, she had very much moved in with him. The cabin at the Evans ranch was officially empty. But neither of them had mentioned it out loud. Luke was too afraid to, just in case she changed her mind and decided to pack up her stuff.

He liked having her stuff there. Damnit, he liked having *her* there.

"Do you have a preference of which one we watch?" Bella collapsed down next to him, laptop wide open and being pushed in his face. "Here. You can choose from the list."

Luke's eyes ran down a long list of titles. Each one darker than the next. A shiver went down his spine as he connected the dots and realized his brother wasn't the only one to go to all of these places. Dangerous places. Bella had too.

"Uh, what about this one?" He pointed. "*Hamburg Hunter.*"

Europe is relatively safe, right?

Bella flashed him a smirk before jumping back up and making her way over to the television. After hooking up the laptop and pressing play, she was back in his arms just a moment later. Snuggled against his chest as he breathed in berries.

Just ten minutes in, his education began. Turns out

Europe wasn't that safe after all. And the "Hamburg hunter" was in fact not a hunting enthusiast as the title implied.

Jesus Christ.

CHAPTER FOURTEEN

Bella was leaving Woodvalley in three days, twelve hours, and thirty-two minutes. When did this countdown start, you ask? Two days and twenty-eight minutes ago to be exact. That was the day that the toe-curling kisses, constant laughter, and mind-blowing sex went from being the best three and a half weeks of her life to her suddenly feeling like she was choking on her heart. Which just so happened to be stuck in her throat.

Not good.

That was an understatement. Sometime between the countdown beginning and her current pacing of Woodvalley's sidewalk, a shockingly loud internal struggle had started, playing tug-of-war with her head and her heart. She wasn't ready for this to be the end. Not her time in Woodvalley. And not with Luke. But just because she felt this way, she was fully aware that it in no way meant Luke felt the same.

Mr. I've Never Had A Relationship was the ultimate bachelor. Or fuckboy, depending on who you were speaking to. The only reason he'd made an exception for her was because they had a deal. She was supposed to leave. And never come back.

It made things kind of tricky. It also made it highly likely that if she attempted a conversation about continuing whatever this was, he would laugh in her face. Or change the locks. Or both.

Goddamnit.

Bella whipped around with enough force that she actually heard air whoosh. But her step faltered as the next whoosh knocked the wind out of her. Her body hit a hard wall of muscle and her eyes were filled with flannel. By the time her head went up to meet a concerned Wade's creased brow, he'd already taken several steps back.

"Bella, you okay? I didn't hurt you, did I? You turned so suddenly."

Great. Way to look like a basket case.

Pacing the town center streets wasn't a good look as it was. Plowing down pedestrians while doing it was even worse.

"Uh, yeah, sorry. I'm fine. Totally fine," she lied.

"Okay," Wade said slowly as he continued to study her, "I was just on my way over to the diner—wanna come grab a cuppa coffee with me?"

It was a pity invite. There was no doubt she looked like an unhinged basket case now.

"Uh, no, I'm fine. Really. I was just on my way to …" *Think. Make something up. Why can't I think of anything?*

"Seriously? That's the best you can do?" Wade chuckled. "Come on, darlin', let's go. Coffee's on me."

Apparently, he wasn't taking no for an answer, and Bella had no energy to put up a fight, so she followed along, both of them quiet until they took a seat in one of the red leather booths in Molly's.

"So," Wade started, "you gonna tell me what's going on?"

"I don't know what you mean." Bella's eyes shot to the menu as she pretended to scan it.

Wade sighed. "Come on, Bella. I know something's up. Is it Luke—did he upset you?"

It was her turn to sigh. When did she become so transparent? She was usually so good at concealing her emotions and hiding her crazy. Luke had broken her.

"No, Luke hasn't upset me. He's ... he's—"

"What can I get ya?"

Saved by the waitress. Buying Bella two whole minutes until she was in the hot seat again.

"He's what?" Wade asked as soon as the waitress disappeared to fetch their drinks.

Urgh. "Look, he's not done anything. That's not the problem. The problem is that ... I think, no, I *know* I've fallen for him." *Oh wow, that's out there now, out loud and everything.*

"And?" Wade didn't even look the slightest bit shocked. Another reminder that she was doing a terrible job of hiding anything.

"And that's bad. Really, really bad. That's not what this was supposed to be. It's not what we agreed."

"And what exactly did you agree?"

"That this is temporary. We have fun for a few weeks, no strings, no commitment. Then I go home. Falling for him wasn't part of the plan." She was so fucked.

Leaning back into the squeaky cushion, Wade took his time studying her. Giving her the opportunity to draw in a few well-earned deep breaths.

"How do you know he's not fallen for you too?"

She shot him a glare. "This isn't a movie, Wade. This is real life. And in real life, women fall for emotionally unavailable men every day, and do you know what happens to these women?" Wade's brow raised, but he didn't reply. "They get their hearts broken. That's me. That's where I'm headed."

She couldn't be sure, but her voice may have risen to crazy lady levels.

"How can you be so sure?" Wade asked, with an annoyingly nonchalant shrug.

"Because I don't have the magical powers needed to change someone. Luke made it very clear to me who he was. And I went there with him anyway. Knowing full well he had the potential to hurt me."

Wade hummed. He carried on humming as the waitress reappeared and placed hot coffee in front of both of them. It was only when they were alone again that she was treated to his musings.

"I think you should tell him how you feel."

"What?"

Was he high? Or has he just not been listening?

Infuriatingly, Wade repeated what he just said and added a "He deserves to know" onto the end.

They went back and forth for a while after that. Bella argued that there wasn't much point unless she was wanting to add humiliation to the whole heartbreak thing. Which she didn't. Whereas Wade was insistent that there was a possibility that Luke returned her feelings. Bella wasn't holding her breath.

By the time they were done, she'd drunk three coffees, had an enormous stack of pancakes, and was so high on caffeine and sugar that she was even more of a nervous wreck than before she'd sat down.

"Please tell me you'll at least think about it?" Wade tried one last time as they each slid out of the booth.

"I told you I would. I'll think about it. But if I decide not to say anything, you're gonna need to respect that." Bella stood and followed Wade toward the exit. "Which means you can't say anything either, Wade. I mean it. This is one friend confiding in another, that's it. Not another piece of gossip you can spread around."

"For the billionth time, I'm not a freaking gossip." She couldn't contain her smile as she looked up at Wade as he shook his head while holding open the door. "I told you, I'm normally the last to know anything going on around here."

"Good. Keep being a hermit, Wade Evans, that way you won't be tempted to tell Luke about our little conversation," Bella said, still grinning as she passed him and returned to the familiar terracotta sidewalk.

"You're secrets safe with me, darlin'." He winked.

God, she hoped that was true.

***

Bella had made a decision. Wade may have influenced said decision. Slightly. But she'd been the one to make it, so she still felt pretty proud. With two days to go before she was supposed to leave and never look back, she was going to tell Luke how she felt. Tonight.

She was feeling good about her decision. Confident. She was in no way watching the clock, counting down the hours of when Luke would be back home from his shift. Well, she might have checked her watch, but only a perfectly normal number of times.

Yeah. Okay.

"He deserves to know," Bella muttered to herself as she entered Luke's mancave.

She referred to it as his mancave frequently, mostly because it annoyed him. But, really, it was just a room at the back of the house where he kept his books, movies, and music collection. And there just so happened to be a pool table in there too.

After scouring the bookshelves in search of something to distract her, Bella settled on a murder mystery. There was nothing like a good "who done it" to pass the time. As she cradled her find to her chest, she swiftly turned toward the door. But a piece of paper hanging off a nearby counter caught her eye and caused her footsteps to falter. A letter. *The* letter. Luke must have been re-reading it. Which was his business. It was just that her name was written. Not just once either, three times to be exact. She could see her name scrawled three fricking times from the other side of the room. What the hell?

Bella was all about respecting privacy and boundaries. She'd kept the letter safe all this time and had never once had the urge to read it. But her name. It was right there.

Mocking her. Three times seemed over the top too for two paragraphs. If it was just the one time she probably wouldn't care.

Wouldn't you?

Okay, she might care a little. But one time wouldn't merit walking over to the pine counter and picking up the paper. Which was exactly what she found herself doing.

Shaky hands lifted as she suppressed her inner voice and read. Not all of it. Just the part that had been screaming at her.

Bella needs help. She's alone. Like we were. I'm the only family she has ever had and if I'm gone, she has no one. I'm scared of that most. I know I have no right to ask this, but I figure that even you wouldn't go against a dead man's wish. And I'm not above emotional manipulation so I'm going to ask. Look after her. Please.

I know it won't be easy. Bella will tell you she's okay, she'll even act like it too. But don't be fooled. She needs you. She needs a friend. I don't care what or how you do it, but while she is there, I need you to form some sort of bond with her. Give Bella something to hold on to. Let her know she's not alone. Introduce her to your friends, their girlfriends, anyone, just give her a safe place to come back to whenever she needs to.

She'd read enough. Uncurling her fingers, she let the paper drop back onto the wooden surface. She felt sick. Had it all been a lie? Their connection. Her new friends, who just so happened to be his friends too. All this time, had she just been a fucking charity case?

No. Luke wouldn't do that. His walls came down just for you. You saw it with your own eyes.

She wanted to believe that. So badly. But the doubts kept coming. The guilt Luke felt and how much it was tearing him up. Her new friendship with the girlfriends of his friends. The insistence on her moving in. Marco's words wouldn't stop echoing. Luke had neatly ticked off each of his brother's requests. Form a bond, check. Introduce her to his friends and their partners, check. Give her a safe place to come back to, check. But the worst one, the one hardest to swallow was that for the first time in a long time, she didn't feel alone.

Fuck.

She needed to get out of there. Her head was starting to spin.

How could I have been so stupid?

Luke had told her from the start. He didn't do relationships. Ever. And he didn't. There she was thinking that this was different. That she was somehow special. That there was a chance that he'd fallen for her like she'd fallen for him. But he hadn't, and she wasn't special. He just felt sorry for her.

Scurrying out of the mancave, she went straight for the stairs and up to the bedroom. She needed to pack.

CHAPTER FIFTEEN

Luke had made up his mind. He was going to ask Bella to stay. And if she didn't want to, then he was going to ask her if they could do long distance for a while. He was finally ready for a relationship. As long as it was with her. If ever there was a woman for him, it was Bella.

As he pulled into his driveway, though, his newfound calmness disappeared and panic set in. Bella's car was next to his, the trunk wide open as she hauled bags inside. Her bags. It didn't take a genius to work out that she was leaving.

Without delay, he was out of his car and stamping stone. Unable to keep his cool. "What the hell is going on?"

The boot of Bella's car slammed shut as her head shot up. But she didn't meet his gaze as she rounded the car. "Um, hey." Why was she not looking at him? "So, I know I was supposed to leave in two days, but something came up."

What the fuck?

"Something came up?" he repeated in a no doubt incredulous tone.

"Yeah." She nodded, mostly at the ground. "A work thing, so, yeah, I've got to get back."

The coldness in Bella's voice was making his chest ache. What on earth had happened between him kissing her goodbye this morning to her packing up her stuff two days early? And why the hell wasn't she looking him in the eye?

Severely lacking patience, he decided to ask just that. But first he needed her eyes. "Angel, look at me?" When she didn't, he tried again. "Please, angel, look at me."

Slowly, silver lifted to meet him. But he didn't recognize what he saw. They were blank. Devoid of any emotion. And it reminded him so much of himself, it scared the shit out of him.

"What happened, where'd you go?" he asked, keeping his tone gentle.

Her stare was still blank. "Look, Luke, it's not a big deal. This thing between us was only ever gonna end one way, anyway. It just needs to end two days early, that's all."

It's not a big deal. Only ever gonna end one way. Was it all in his head? He was so sure she felt it too. He felt sick. Who even was this woman before him; where had Bella gone?

Maybe this was her all along?

That couldn't be true, could it? He wanted to shake her. Find out what she'd done with the woman he'd fallen for. But he didn't get a chance. This Bella was done. And she was climbing into the driver's seat without a second look.

He had to stop her. Which is what he tried to do next as he clung onto the door she was trying to shut.

"What the fuck, Bella?"

Another look he'd never seen before hit him full force in the stomach. "Luke, please. I need to get on the road, it's a long drive."

That was her main concern? Driving times.

Now he was really pissed.

"Fine. By all means, *get on the road.* But before you do, you mind telling me why you were about to leave without saying goodbye? Or maybe you wanna tell me why whatever it is that has *come up* can't wait another two days?"

"Why do you care?"

More frost hit his veins.

"What?" He just didn't get it.

"I said, why do you care? This thing between us was temporary, remember? That's the only reason you let it go this far, right, 'cause I'm leaving?" She didn't wait for a reply. "So it ended two days early, so fucking what? I'm sure some more nameless sex will help you forget pretty damn quickly. Why don't you get on that?"

Bella tried to tug at the car door again, but he kept his grip firm as he tried to process her words.

"What's going on with you? Where's the Bella I left this morning … in my bed?"

"She's right here. Saying goodbye." He searched her for clues. Signs. Anything that would help him decide what to do, what to say. But just like him, when she wanted her expression blanked, she knew exactly how to do it.

Fight for her. Make her stay.

But he couldn't. Because what was the point? She was right. They had an agreement. This thing between them had an end date. And it was the only reason he had opened up to her in the first place. Even if something had happened that had made her want to leave, she'd made up her mind. And God knows he'd been through this enough to know how things went from here. She was just one of a long line of people that didn't want him.

He didn't bother hiding how he felt this time though. He let her see it all. Anger. Pain. Hurt. But it was the disappointment that stung the most as he slammed her car door shut and walked away.

How could I have been so fucking stupid?

***

It had been two days since Bella left. Ironically, today was the day she originally intended on leaving. Which was probably why his phone was blowing up. He might not have told anyone that Bella was gone. Anyone being his friends and their women. He also might not have shown up at work these past few days.

For someone who was pretty damn used to abandonment, he was taking this latest rejection particularly badly. As in, he was surprised he hadn't needed his stomach pumped.

There's still time.

A heavy bang on his front door had him groaning as his head began to throb again. He'd ignored the doorbell for the past five minutes, so what made whoever it was outside think he was about to get his ass off the couch now, he didn't know.

The phone on his trunk table started ringing out, which only made him groan again as he threw his head back into the cushion.

Why? Just leave me alone for fucks sake.

More bangs and more ringing went on for a good few minutes until he heard something even more disturbing. His front door opening and closing.

What the fuck?

Hunter, his gigantic friend, strolled into his living room seconds later. Not saying a word, a nonchalant expression on that big ugly face as he sat himself down on one of Luke's leather couches. His friend shot him an expectant look, as if he was the one who owed him answers.

The goddamn cheek.

"How the fuck did you get in here?"

"Keys," Hunter grunted. "Why haven't you been at work?"

"*Keys?*" Luke repeated sarcastically. "And where the hell did you get my fucking *keys?*"

Hunter ignored Luke's question and repeated his own. It went on like that for a while. Luke had almost forgotten how stubborn his friend was. Too bad he was more stubborn. Which is why they ended up sitting in silence. For a really long time.

In that time, much to Luke's annoyance, Hunter had gotten up, gone to the kitchen, and made himself a sandwich. His friend really was taking the piss today.

"You gonna sit there all day?" Luke snarled as he reached for the half-empty whiskey bottle decorating his coffee table.

"Depends. You gonna tell me what's going on?"

Luke was done. The sooner Hunter got the hell out, the better. So after a rather large swig of his drink, he announced, "She's gone."

Hunter calmly nodded and threw in a "Yup."

Fucking hell.

"What do you mean *yup*? You've been waiting all day for me to tell you what my problem is, and now I've said it, you're not interested? What the fuck, man?"

His friend had the audacity to tut at him. "I know she's gone. She was always gonna go, right? I'm more interested in finding out what the fuck you're gonna do about it?"

"What are you talking about?" Luke's eyes narrowed on the big man.

"You *know* what I'm talking about. But fine, I'll play ball. Why don't you go on ahead and tell me the reason you're skipping work and drowning your sorrows?"

Luke didn't answer, he simply glared.

"'Cause she's gone, right?" His ex-friend continued, "I told you weeks ago not to be one of those guys who forgets to pull his head outta his ass, didn't I? Right. So what the hell is it still doing up there, dumbass?"

The last thing Luke needed was a roasting. And he definitely didn't need to pull his head out of his ass. He was the injured party here. Not Bella. Him. She rejected him. So his friend really needed to stop giving him shit. Right now.

"Enough." Luke scowled as he saw Hunter readying to run his mouth again. "Bella ended it. I was on my way home to tell her I was all in, but she wasn't interested. *She* left *me*."

They both fell into silence after that. What else was there to say? Luke decided to go back to his whiskey. He wasn't nearly as numb as he wanted to be yet.

"Did you tell her?" Hunter asked, a while later.

"What?" Luke didn't bother hiding the impatience in his voice. He was so ready to drink in peace.

"That you were all in, did you tell her that? How did that

conversation play out?"

Again with the questions.

What does this man want from me, a fucking recording of me getting my heart ripped out?

Luke slammed his bottle against the table as he twisted to face Hunter. He wanted his friend to see everything, starting with how much he was pissing him off.

"She told me something *came up*. That she had to leave early. If I hadn't come home when I did, she would've left without a word," he said through gritted teeth. "When I tried to talk to her, she set me straight, told me that we had an agreement. It was always gonna end like this. Her leaving two days early didn't make a difference." Saying the words out loud brought back the gut wrench.

Hunter hummed. "So, you didn't tell her how you feel?"

"Are you not fucking listening to me? She was gonna fucking leave without saying goodbye!" His voice was rising, but he couldn't control it, didn't want to. "She basically told me that everything that happened between us happened 'cause there was an end date and that I should go fuck someone else." His leg was bouncing now, anger and pain rolling off him in waves as he fought to reign himself in. "I fucking love her," he roared. "I let her in. See all of me. Told her shit I've never even said out loud before. And what does she do? I'll tell you what she does, she does what everyone fucking does … she left."

He didn't need a therapist to know that he had abandonment issues, he was all too aware. But unlike his past rejection, he didn't know how he was supposed to recover from this.

"Luke, not everyone leaves—" Hunter's voice had gentled, but he didn't have a chance to get much more out before Luke's humorless laugh filled the room.

"This is why I don't bother. This is why it's easier to keep people at arm's length. I promised myself I'd never let anyone do this to me again. I fucking promised." His head fell into his hands, despair now seeping out of every pore.

"I'm such a fucking idiot."

Luke went quiet after that. Taking comfort in the darkness as his hands continued to cup his face. He didn't know how much time passed, but it was long enough to forget he had an audience. It was only when his friend sucked in a deep breath that he remembered he was there.

Already preparing himself for his next lecture, Luke was surprised when one didn't come. He waited. Then waited some more. But, still, nothing. When he finally lifted his head, Hunter's usual gruff exterior had softened. And something a bit like understanding creased his face.

"What?" Luke asked. "Why are you looking at me like that? Just say what you need to say."

Luke watched as Hunter slowly leaned forward, his elbows coming to his knees. "You need to tell her."

It wouldn't make a difference.

Almost as if he'd heard him, Hunter spoke again. "You need to lay it all out for her. She could be making her decision based on fear ... so give her some facts. You owe it to her, and yourself."

Luke wanted to protest. Tell Hunter he was talking out of his ass. But Luke couldn't. Annoyingly, his friend was making sense. Luke hadn't actually told her how he felt. Not that he planned on declaring his love the night she left. But the fact remained that he did love her. And she should know.

Don't let her be another regret.

No more regrets. Life was too short.

You're really going to do this?

The decision had already been made. If he was going to get his heart ripped out, then he was going to do it properly.

CHAPTER SIXTEEN

Apartment hunting sucked. Apartment hunting while shards of your heart rattled around your rib cage, sucked more. Throw in the fact Bella was technically in between jobs and the pickings were beyond slim.

It had been five whole days since she'd left Woodvalley, and she'd made zero progress on finding somewhere to live. Which meant she was still staying in her crappy motel and would likely be there for a while. And it *was* crappy. And depressing. This place could give the DMV a run for its money.

At least it matches your mood.

She supposed that was true. She felt like shit. So she might as well stay somewhere shit too. Bask in the shitness.

As she began channel flicking for the millionth time that night, her phone buzzed against the laminated wood on the bedside table. She didn't need to check who it was. The same three people had been calling for the past three days: Libby, Cat, and Rachel. She was yet to answer. Luke had also called, but only once. Two days after she'd left. She obviously didn't answer that call either, knowing no good was going to come of it. But it didn't stop her from obsessing over it. Wondering what he was going to say.

The vibrating stopped only to start again a moment later. That was different. Usually Libby, Cat, or Rachel would try only once. It was different enough to have Bella leaning over to grab her phone. But when she saw the name on the screen, she was starting to wish she hadn't.

Luke. Why was he calling?

Maybe answer it and find out?

That would be ludicrous. There was no way she was answering. But that didn't stop her stomach from churning at the sight of his name. Or her chest pounding. Eventually, his name disappeared. The new heart palpitations were sticking around though.

Bella stared at the screen, frozen. It was only when his name popped up again that she blinked. This time, he'd sent a message. Ignoring her shaky fingers, she slid open the text. Heart still racing at a worrying pace.

Luke: *Answer the phone, Bella, we need to talk.*

As soon as she'd read it, her phone was back to ringing.

"Shit," she muttered under her breath, realizing her read notifications were switched on and Luke now knew that she'd seen his message.

Answer it.

No. There was nothing to say. She needed to be logical. She was never going to get over him, if she kept thinking about him. Talking led to thinking. Thinking led to missing. And missing would lead to Bella doing something stupid, like driving back to Woodvalley and declaring her love.

Love?

Not now brain. There was no time to think as the ringing stopped and another text appeared.

Luke: *Seriously, Bella, answer your phone.*

She was not going to answer her phone. No matter how badly her heart hurt, she would not forgo her dignity. She wasn't anyone's charity case.

***

What am I doing?

Downloading a dating app whilst trying to patch your heart back together with crazy glue was indeed a questionable decision. Going on an actual date with somebody from said app was just plain dumb.

She'd known as soon as she'd arrived at the restaurant that it was a bad idea. But it was too late. It's not like she could stand the guy up. Just because she was hurting, it didn't mean she had the right to hurt someone else. So there she sat, in Guac and Wrap, on the worst date of her life. Possibly even the worst date of anyone's life.

The fact that the man looked nothing like his profile picture was the least of her worries. No. It was his unusual lifestyle, which was the real kicker. Straight away, before even saying hello, he'd informed her that he was a fruitarian. Something that until forty long minutes ago, Bella would have believed was totally made up. But no, apparently, this is a thing. A thing, Darren had been kind enough to explain to her. In great detail.

Oh joy.

So far, she'd learned about the very many benefits a fruit-based diet has on the digestive system. The anti-aging properties in fruit that basically makes you immortal. And oh, yes, her favorite, the ignorance of society as a whole.

Bet you're wishing you stood him up now, right?

Maybe. Okay. Definitely. He'd ordered six different mocktails already, while she'd waited all damn day for a frigging taco. Why he'd suggested a Mexican restaurant when he didn't eat anything on the menu, she had no idea.

A cruel joke?

"See, most people don't know how many varieties of fruit there actually are." Was it Bella, or was Darren looking more and more like a fruitcake? "And you can order them all online, you don't need to rely on what the local supermarkets supply anymore. It's revolutionary."

Bella offered him a tight smile and a polite nod before guzzling down more of her raspberry punch.

Stupid mocktail. If ever there was a time for alcohol, it's right fucking now.

"I order in bulk, whatever I don't freeze, I keep in

drawers around my apartment. Most of it can last a while at room temperature. Bananas ... they can last for a long time."

So his drawers are full of bananas?

Oh God, she was dying. There was no way she'd be able to make it through another freaking mocktail with this lunatic.

"Listen"—Darren's expression turned serious—"Belle."

"Bella," she corrected.

"Right. Bella. So, like, you seem like a cool chick and everything, but I'm gonna be honest and put it all out there. I don't really see this working out." After gesturing between them, he leaned further into the table. "I just don't feel that kind of connection with you, that sexual energy, if you know what I mean."

He's rejecting me?!

This was a whole new low. Even for her. Banana man could do better.

She didn't bother to reply. There were no words. Instead, she stood, threw down some money for the mocktails, and did what she should have done forty minutes ago, walked away.

This was all Luke's fault. His call last night had messed with her head. Made it all fuzzy. And scared the hell out of her. Enough that she'd downloaded the first dating app she'd come across in an attempt to stop him from infiltrating her every thought. Of course it hadn't worked. Even through the fruit chat she'd found herself thinking about him. And the sarcastic tongue-lashing he'd have no doubt administered.

As she climbed into her car, she realized then that there would be no shortcuts to healing. Getting over Luke was going to be slow and painful. And she needed to accept that.

Pulling out her phone, she scrolled to the dating app and pressed *Delete.*

Enough.

It was time to deal with it like an adult. She was going

straight to the supermarket. She needed ice cream, some chips, and between ten and fifty chocolate bars.

Like an adult.

CHAPTER SEVENTEEN

Luke was starting to rethink his genius plan. Waiting outside a dodgy motel for hours wasn't the best idea. He discovered that when he was approached by a woman, who, let's just say, was renting her room by the hour. But he had no choice. This was where Bella was staying according to Cat, who, he'd since learned, had all their locations on her phone. Mr. Dragon Tattoo at the front desk had also confirmed it, and after some convincing, had directed him to room twelve, but there was no answer. So there he stood, waiting.

For how long though?

That was a good question. He'd been there three hours already and there was no sign of her. Where was she? For someone who claimed to have no friends and no life outside of Marco, she sure as hell was making the most of her Saturday night.

Then a godawful thought popped into his head: What if she was with another man?

No. She couldn't be. Right?

Oh how he hoped that wasn't the case. It had only been six days. As soon as he'd pulled his head out of his ass, he'd gone about getting time off work before spending two days driving out there. He was trusting his gut. Trusting that she felt the same way about him as he did about her. She was just scared.

Scared, he could work with. He'd realized something this week. He and Bella were the same. So afraid their shitty childhood would catch up with them, they did the only thing they knew, they ran. Bella had made it further across the world, of course, but he'd definitely mastered the art of running without having to leave town.

Checking his watch again, he let out a sigh. It was ten. If she was out with friends, then it was possible she wouldn't be back for a few more hours.

God-fucking-damnit.

Just as he was contemplating renting his own room, a car pulled up. A blue Prius. This was it. It was go time.

Straightening up, he took a deep breath and watched Bella climb out of the driver's seat, shopping bag in hand. She was alone. *Thank fuck.* And she hadn't noticed him just yet. Luke took a moment to appreciate those precious seconds as he drank her in. God, he'd missed her. When she left, she left him feeling empty. But now that she stood before him, he was beginning to feel whole again.

She's turned you into a soppy bastard.

She had. And he was hoping his new soppy side would be enough to win her back.

"Luke." Bella stopped mid-stride, her mouth actually dropping open at the sight of him.

"Bella," he returned. Their gazes locking. "Hi."

"*Hi,*" she mimicked, not looking impressed at all. "That's all you have to say? What are you doing here? How did you find me?"

"Why'd you leave?" Desperation might have found its way into his voice.

"What are you doing here?" she asked again, ignoring his question.

"I'm here 'cause we're not done. We *can't* be done."

More head shakes. That wasn't good.

His chest heaved and his palms began to sweat as he waited for Bella to reply. A reply that didn't come as her gaze darted to the ground.

"Where were you tonight?" he asked, in the hope it would get her talking.

Her head whipped up at the question, silver narrowing on him. A look of pure defiance on her angelic face as she announced, "I was on a date."

That was a shot straight to the heart. So powerful he stumbled back.

She was on a date?!

Luke's eyes traveled down her outfit. She looked stunning. A short, pale blue dress that resembled a shirt. The first few buttons were open, showing off the top of her lacy black bra. He felt sick at the thought of her wearing that dress for another man. How could she have been on a date? It had been six days. Six fucking days.

He needed a minute. And he took it, turning his back to her and palming his face. But the long, slow exhales weren't working. He was angry. And he couldn't shake it.

Twisting back around, he let her see exactly what those words had done to him. "You went on a fucking date?"

"Yes, Luke." She easily matched his volume. "I went on a fucking date. I'm sorry if that hurts your precious male ego, but that's where I was."

"You think that's okay? Jesus, Bella, you were in my fucking bed six days ago."

"Don't give me that bullshit, Luke," she snapped. "And don't act like I'm betraying you either. You're the one who doesn't do relationships, remember? The only reason you were even with me in the first place was because I was leaving. And that's what I did, like we planned." *Like we planned, my ass.* "So don't you dare stand there and act like the fucking victim."

Next thing he knew, she was on the move, making a beeline for the door, being careful to circle around him. As soon as she was close enough, his hand shot out and went to her arm.

"Bella." His voice may have gentled, but he was running on pure adrenaline. "Please. Stop. Just talk to me. Please."

"There's nothing to say." Her misty eyes told him differently.

"There's a lot to fucking say, angel."

He took comfort in the fact that she wasn't hiding from him. Not like the day she left. He could see every single emotion flicker on her beautiful face. Sadness, anger, pain, all before switching back to rage.

"No, Luke." She wrenched her arm, freeing her from his hold. "I don't wanna hear it. I'm not some box to check off to make you feel less guilty about your dead brother. I do just fine on my own. So go home, Luke."

What the hell is she talking about?

Which is what he asked next. Her reply only confusing him more.

"I'm talking about the letter, Luke. You know, the one Marco left you? I'm not some fucking charity case. I don't need you or your friends. I've done just fine without you for thirty years, and I'll do fine for another thirty."

Keys went to the front door next and a moment later she was pushing open the crimson wood. As soon as she took a step inside, he followed, not giving her a chance to slam the door in his face. They weren't done.

"Hey!" Bella protested as she shoved at his chest. "I mean it, Luke. We're done. Go home."

"We're not done, sweetheart. Not until you tell me what the fuck you're talking about. Are you seriously telling me you left because of something you read in that letter?"

Her eyes were all over him. Searching his face. Looking for something. He let her look. She could do what she wanted if it meant she wasn't trying to push him out the door.

She stayed quiet, even as she launched her shopping bag onto the bedside table and collapsed down onto the mattress. When her head dropped into her hands, he was moving. Dropping to his knees before her, wrapping his own hands around hers.

"Angel," he soothed, "Please, talk to me. Help me

understand what happened."

Luke was trying his best to think back to what was in the letter. He remembered Marco had written a few lines about Bella. Something about her being his best friend and asking Luke to look out for her. Could that be what she was talking about? If he was honest, the part of the letter he'd been focused on and had found himself re-reading over and over again was the part about how they shared the same mother.

Her hands dropped and watery eyes met his. "You really don't know?"

"I really don't know," he confirmed. "That letter, Bella, he … he wanted me to know that we weren't half brothers like I thought. My mom was his mom. All this time I thought my dad was just some guy who got my mom pregnant, I had no idea that they were together. That at some point they were a family."

Bella's eyes widened; she'd obviously not read that part. He realized then that he should have told her. That was the reason he'd been struggling. He regretted that now. She deserved to know everything.

"But … but Marco asked you to look after me. Form a bond. Make your friends and their girlfriends be my friends too." *He did? Fuck. Yeah, he did.* It was all coming back now.

"You honestly think that's what this was?" He let his hands cup her face as he looked into her. A small nod gave him his answer and tore at his heart. "Sweetheart, I would never." His nose nudged hers as he took a deep inhale of berries. "This is real. I think deep down you know that. Otherwise, you wouldn't have run."

"He told you to form a bond with me—introduce me to your friends, their girlfriends …" She trailed off.

"Think about it, angel. *Really* think about it. In the four weeks you've known me, do I strike you as the kind of guy to spend time with someone if I didn't want to? And if you think for one second I have any kind of control over Libby, Cat, and Rachel, then you obviously don't know them well enough."

She needed to believe him. Believe that this was real. *They* were real.

Pulling back slightly, their eyes met, and his heart raced. It was time. He had to tell her. It was now or never.

"You made me promise not to fall in love with you, Bella," he said softly, "but I broke that promise, angel." Moisture pooled in her eyes as their heavy breaths echoed around the room. "I fell. And I fell hard. I love you, Bella." When she didn't reply, he said it again. "Did you hear me, sweetheart? I've fallen in love with you."

Those tears that had been threatening to spill just moments ago, finally broke free, a steady stream trickling down rosy cheeks. Using his shaky hands, he began thumbing them away.

"You can't." She sniffed. "You don't mean that."

Enough talking. She wasn't listening. He needed to show her. Launching forward, his mouth took hers, opening her to him and swiping inside until the taste of sweet berries tingled his tongue. Urgency laced every movement as he greedily feasted on her. In turn, her own hands came to his head, impatient fingers raking through his hair and tugging him closer.

Pushing up from the carpet, he eased Bella back, lowering her onto the bed and positioning himself above her. He only broke their connection once, to tell her "I love you," before letting his weight hit his elbows as he kissed her again. Hard.

Swallowing each other's moans, they kissed until both their bodies shook. It was only when Bella's hands went to the hem of his shirt, that he let go of her lips. She was yanking up the material, letting her fingers skim over his stomach, leaving scorch marks all over his skin as fire raged within.

Helping her lift the shirt over his head, he lost her mouth, but used it as an opportunity to tell her "I love you" again. It was okay that she wasn't replying. She didn't need to. She just needed to hear it. He'd say it over and over again until she believed him. No matter how long it took.

Her expert fingers unbuttoning his jeans and pulling down the zipper was her only answer. One he'd happily take. She was pushing down his pants and boxers next, freeing him, before flipping them over until she was on top.

"I love you," he repeated through labored breaths, his eyes not wavering from hers as her fingers went to the buttons on her dress.

He watched her swallow hard. But no words left her pouty red lips. Instead, her dress hit the floor, then her bra, and before he knew it, her panties were being pushed to one side as she lowered herself onto him.

"I love you," he rasped, his eyes squeezing shut, his head arching.

Jesus Christ, she felt perfect. A roar ripped through him as she slowly lifted herself before dropping back down again. Then she did it again. Each time, lifting up a bit further before slamming back down until he could no longer see straight, let alone think straight.

He managed one more "I love you" before everything became hazy.

CHAPTER EIGHTEEN

Bella stared down at her now empty coffee cup. The stench of fried eggs and bacon clogging her throat as she let tears skim her cheeks. She'd done exactly what Luke had accused her of doing last night. She'd run. Snuck out of bed and driven to the nearest roadside diner. She hadn't even waited until sunlight.

Hearing Luke tell her he loved her, over and over, had done something to her. Toppled down the very last defenses she'd surrounded her heart with. And that was beyond scary. She'd promised herself a long time ago to never let that happen. Marco was the closest she'd ever come to loving a man, but she'd given herself that, that was safe. That love wouldn't hurt her. Not like Luke's love would.

So why did you sleep with him?

Her hand went to her face as she began swiping the tears away. That was a good question. She clearly couldn't trust herself around him. Yet another reason she'd run.

"Another coffee, doll?" the young waitress cast a sympathetic glance her way.

Bella gave her a nod, keeping her gaze on the mug as a steady stream of hot liquid filled her vision.

Even after the waitress left, she continued to stare.

Doubt was creeping in. Making her body heavy, her chest tight and her throat restrict.

Just as she was contemplating calling an ambulance, peppery leather filled her lungs. No longer spellbound by the coffee, her eyes shot up. Luke.

Fuck.

She'd not run far enough.

Or maybe you wanted to be found.

"Angel." His serious stare was killing her. She'd hurt him. Again. "Please stop running."

She was shaking her head in denial, but she couldn't quite bring herself to deny it out loud.

Because he's right. You're running. That's what you do best.

"People can't hurt you if they can't find you," she whispered.

"I'm not going to hurt you, angel."

"You will." Her words were still quiet, her tone resigned.

"No, Bella." Luke reached across the table and grasped each of her hands, squeezing them tight as he looked so deep into her, she was finding it hard to swallow. "I'd hurt myself and the whole fucking world before I ever hurt you, that I promise."

She wanted to believe him. So badly. But fuckboys didn't magically turn into princes overnight. The man had never once had a relationship and now all of a sudden he was in love. What made her so special? It was impossible to wrap her head around it.

"Why me?" she asked.

A look of confusion crossed Luke's face. "What?"

"I said, *why me?* You've been with plenty of women." She pushed down the nausea those words conjured. "What makes you think, after all this time, you're ready to be with someone … ready to love someone? Ready to love me?"

He squeezed her hands again. "Sweetheart, how are you not getting this?" A small smile tipped his lips.

"Getting what?" she dared ask.

"No other woman was *you*. I've been waiting my whole

life for *you*, Bella. Don't you get it?" She was held hostage by the flames dancing in his eyes. They thickened the air, made it crackle. "You were right about the walls I put up. Nothing short of a bulldozer would get them to crumble. I made sure of that. But I realize now that they've been falling ever since the day I met you. And now there's nothing left. They fell. For you. So I could love you the way you're meant to be loved."

That was a good fucking answer. Back was the chest pain. Only this time, she was finding it hard to breathe. It wasn't helping that his intense gaze was still boring into her. Expectantly.

What the hell am I supposed to say to that?

Luckily, she didn't have to reply, not yet anyway, as he continued to shock her into submission.

"Move in with me?"

"Huh?" was all she could manage.

"Move in with me," he repeated. "Come back to Woodvalley."

"You're insane."

"Insanely in love." His smile was now full-blown. "Come on, angel. Move in with me."

The man's cockiness never failed to shock her; she hadn't even told him she loved him back. She had even run from him. Twice. And yet here he was, asking her to move in. After knowing her for the grand total of four weeks.

But you do love him, don't you?

Nothing could stop the sigh from leaving her lips. She did love him, it was true. But that didn't mean Luke wasn't acting certifiable, which is what she told him.

"What have you got to lose?" was his reply.

"Everything."

"Or nothing? Look me in the eyes and tell me you don't love me." *Oh shit.* She couldn't. Wouldn't. And he knew it. Was using it against her. "Come on, angel. What are you waiting for?"

"Fine!" she might have yelled. "Fine. I love you, okay,

Luke." She was getting louder. "Are you happy? I said it. I love you, and I'm scared shitless you have the power to hurt me more than anyone else ever could."

"What did you say?" he panted.

She couldn't tell if he was being serious or not, so she didn't answer. Not that he waited for her to. He was sliding out of the booth and tugging her out of her seat a moment later, his hand going to her waist, easily pulling her into him as he searched her expression.

"You love me?"

"Yes," she breathed. Heart hammering.

Suddenly, his mouth was on her. Kissing the hell out of her. Scrambling her senses. A kiss so good, it had her questioning everything.

What's a little pain if it means getting to kiss this man every day?

Reluctantly, she pulled back, letting her eyes roam his face. "Don't hurt me."

"Never," he boomed, "I swear, angel. Your heart is safe with me."

This time, she was the one to capture his lips. Hoping to find the answer on the tip of his tongue, she took her time tasting him. Not stopping as her spine tingled and his hoarse groan vibrated down her throat.

Her mind raced quicker than her pulse. Could she really do this?

You were considering it a week ago. Before you even knew he loved you.

She needed to hear that. Be reminded that seven days ago she was all in. After last night, she was no longer questioning his intentions. She needed to stop making excuses. Face her fear. And follow her heart.

Coming up for air once again, she let her forehead drop against his. "Let's do this. Let's move in together."

She didn't need to look to know that he was smiling. The light laugh tickling her lips was enough. He was yet to answer, though, he was too busy burying his hands under her arms. A moment later, she was off the floor and being spun around by strong arms.

Whistles and hoots from other diners erupted around them. Her own giggle even escaped as happiness bloomed in her belly. For the first time in her life, she was going to run toward something, instead of away. And she knew deep down to her soul that Luke was worth it. He was worth the risk.

EPILOGUE

Two weeks later

Bella stared at the pink troll doll sitting on Luke's living room shelf. It looked so wrong. His place was all classy and sleek. *She* was not classy *or* sleek. And nor were her things. *Clearly.*

Since she'd moved in, Luke had insisted Bella put her belongings out on display. Which she did. The only problem was her belongings consisted mostly of random, garish trinkets she'd picked up on her travels. And they so did not go with his decor. Which she told him. Again and again. But did he care? Nope.

"Angel." Luke sighed, appearing from the kitchen. "Not this again."

Bella whipped around to face him, arms still crossed, frown still firmly in place. "It just looks silly."

He flashed her a sexy lopsided smile. "I like having your things out. It makes the place feel more like a home."

She turned back to the shelf to pick up her bright blue shark bottle opener. She'd snagged it in Sydney. Shark in hand, she began waving it at Luke. "This? This makes your place feel more like a home?"

"This"—he quickly swiped the bottle opener from her—"this is a part of you, angel. A part of your life. Which means I love it. And I want to look at it every day. And for the millionth time, it's not *my* place, it's *ours*."

"You love the shark?" she asked incredulously. She was not convinced.

"I love the shark." He grinned.

"And the troll doll?"

"And the troll doll," he repeated, a short laugh leaving his lips.

"And the—"

He cut her off, taking her hand, pulling her into him, and covering her mouth. "I'm gonna save us time and tell you that I love them all. Everything, sweetheart."

She shot him a look. The one that called bullshit. Even with her mouth covered, she was pretty sure she was pulling it off.

"Do you know why I kitted this place out with designer shit and fancy gadgets?"

James Bond fan?

She had no idea. Her mouth was still covered, so her smartass reply was out, which meant she could only shake her head. She realized, a moment later, was for the best as his expression grew more serious.

"Growing up," he continued, "I never had anything nice. Anything expensive. I had nothing but the clothes on my back. I'm sure you can relate." *Yup.* "Well, when I started earning, I promised myself that my life would be different from now on. Where I lived would be clean. I'd own nice things. And most importantly, I wanted a home. I'd never had one before. No one had ever given me that chance."

He was breaking her heart.

"So I saved. I worked my ass off. And I bought this place. Filled it with fancy shit. Got a cleaner to come every week. But do you know the one thing I couldn't buy? The one thing this place is missing?" He dropped his hand then, his dark gaze boring into her, waiting for her to speak.

"A troll doll?" a playful smile started to spread.

"No, Bella." Luke's smile was back and so was the

twinkle in his eyes. "*You*. You were the one thing this place was missing. You were the missing piece. The key to making it a home."

She was beaming now. Happiness warming her insides and hope blooming in her chest. "Okay, okay, I'll leave the troll doll out. You win."

Wrapping her hands around his neck, she gave him a tug until his head dropped. She wasted no time pulling him into a kiss. A kiss that made everything worth it.

***

Six weeks later

Bella was back at the Evans ranch, and it felt surreal. Three months ago, she'd driven up this very driveway, completely unaware that by doing so, her life would be forever changed. But in a good way of course. Hence, the humongous smile on her face as Luke tagged her hand and led them up to the main house.

Tonight, was Zach and Libby's rehearsal dinner. Tomorrow, they would be getting married. And Bella could not wait. She'd never, ever, ever been to a wedding before.

Because you've never had any friends.

Right. No friends meant no wedding invites. But now she had actual living friends, and they were all dying to get married. Jackpot.

"Wade!" she squealed as she dropped Luke's hand and ran into her friend's arms.

Wade had to be her favorite of all her newfound friends. And it wasn't because she'd gotten to know him outside of her relationship with Luke either. There was just something so calming about the man. He kind of reminded her of a little old lady, not that she'd ever tell him that. He just had all of those quirky traits, like wisdom, kindness, and let's not forget, massive freaking gossip. Oh, and he was big on home comforts too, which meant the man hardly ever left the ranch. One of the reasons, Bella guessed, why he was still single.

"Well, hello to you too, darlin'." Wade chuckled.

"Oh, don't mind me," Luke teased, raising his hands in the air, "you just go on right ahead and start throwing yourself at other men."

"Well, if you'd have bought that cowboy hat, like I asked you to … maybe I wouldn't have to go looking for it elsewhere." She shot Luke a wink.

Despite his laughter, he was pulling her out of Wade's embrace moments later and plastering her to his side. Such a caveman.

You love it.

She did.

"Come on, Wade, take us to the alcohol." She gestured for him to lead the way.

As requested, he took them to the back of the house where a huge tent had been erected. Off to the side was a bar with so many bottles of booze, she felt her liver twitch. It was going to be a good night.

As they gathered around the bar, and Luke went about making her a drink, she noticed Wade's attention drift. Not just drift but leave the party entirely. Instead, he fixated on the house. Bella followed his gaze, all the way over to a petite, dark-haired woman dragging a huge laundry bag through the backdoor.

"Who's that?" she asked.

When he didn't reply, she felt her smile spread as she asked again. This time Wade jolted, shaking his head before turning his attention back to Bella.

"What?"

"I said … who's the woman? You know, the one you're making goo-goo eyes at?"

"Darlin', I ain't making goo-goo eyes at anyone; I don't even know what goo-goo eyes are."

Just as she was about to reply, the woman reappeared. She'd lost the bag and had emerged from the house carrying a stack of folded towels. Bella looked at Wade. Yep, just like she thought, his gaze was back on the woman.

"Ah ha!" She pointed accusingly. "You're doing it again!" She could practically see the hearts in his eyes. "You *like* her!"

"Bella," Wade warned.

"You *love* her!" She giggled. This was awesome. She might not even need alcohol at this rate. "Come on, who is she?"

"If I tell you, will you promise to stop?"

Not a chance. "Sure, so?"

Wade let out a heavy sigh. "She's the new live-in maid. My brothers hired her a week ago—her name's Riley."

"You asked her out yet?" Bella wasn't taking the dirty look he was giving her personally.

His glare and lack of any real reply told her he hadn't. So she decided to take matters into her own hands.

"Riley?" she shouted across the yard. Then shouted again, ignoring Wade's hand that was now gripping her arm. "Riley?"

The woman's head whipped to Bella, and the deer-in-headlights look she was giving her almost made her feel guilty. But not enough to stop her from gesturing her over.

"Bella," Wade scowled, "what the hell are you doing?"

Bella fluttered her lashes at her friend. "Don't worry, I'm not gonna declare your undying love to the woman."

As soon as Riley was near, she felt Wade stiffen. Actually go stiff. She never thought she'd see the day that the most laid-back Evans brother would go from calm and collected to a tightly wound spring. In an instant.

She got it though. The closer the woman was, the more beautiful she became. Shiny, straight dark hair was pulled into a neat bun. Black-rimmed glasses framed a delicate heart-shaped face. Even the jeans and tee she was wearing tugged at her curves in all the right places. No wonder Wade was captivated.

"Hey," she greeted the very confused-looking woman,

"I'm Bella. Nice to meet you." Riley managed a "Hi" before Bella continued. "Wade mentioned that you started at the ranch a week ago, does that mean you're new in town?"

"Um, yeah." Riley shyly nodded.

"Me too," Bella offered up a warm smile. "I moved here a few months ago, so I'm still getting the lay of the land, so to speak. Maybe we could hang out sometime?"

"Uh—" She'd scared her. But she wasn't done yet. Besides, she was getting good at making friends, and you could never have too many. "Yeah. Sure."

"Amazing, what are you doing tomorrow?" Bella ignored Wade's kick to the ankle. "Wanna come to a wedding?"

This was going to be fun. Who said small towns were boring?

SNEAK PEEK AT BOOK FIVE IN THE LOVE BURNS SERIES

Giddy Up

Riley actually gulped. What on earth was Wade Evans doing here? Outside her staff-issued trailer, flashing those goddamn dimples at her and turning her mind to mush.

Like it wasn't mush before he showed up?

Okay. Fine. So it was plenty mushy already. It had been ever since yesterday afternoon when she'd been strong-armed into attending Zach's wedding. Zach was the oldest of the four Evans brothers. But he didn't work on the ranch like the others. Wade did though. He also just so happened to be the second oldest brother and the man in charge around here. And Riley's brand spanking new boss.

Where the hell is Bella?

That was a good fucking question. Bella was the woman Riley had met yesterday and was responsible for the forementioned strong-arming. Where was she? She hadn't signed up to be harassed by dimples.

"Did you hear me, darlin'?" Wade drawled, this time tipping up his cream Stetson with one finger. "Bella's running late, so you're gonna have to make do with me as your escort."

Oh, she'd heard him alright. Hence the near catastrophic throb in her ears. This was the problem with social anxiety, how was she supposed to tell people she had it if her mouth was too dry to make sounds? It also didn't help that Wade of all people was stood there. Staring. It was difficult enough to talk to regular people, but put a six-foot two, hard-bodied, blue-eyed cowboy in front of her and there was a strong possibility she may never speak again.

"Riley?" He prompted.

Say something. Anything.

"B-But ..."

Jesus Christ.

This didn't bode well for the rest of the day.

Her head shook and her eyes hit the ground. This was embarrassing. Stupidly, she'd thought she could do this. She'd even got dressed up. And swapped her glasses for contact lenses.

Idiot.

"Hey," Wade's hand shot out, and the next thing she knew, a cautious finger was under her chin and lifting her gaze to his. "You okay?"

Nope. Absolutely not.

Another gulp. Her instincts were telling her to run and hide. She couldn't though. Not just because there was nowhere to run to. But because Wade was her boss. And she really needed this job. Which meant, she couldn't just shut the door, she'd have to use actual words to try and get out of this.

Frigging marvellous.

"I, uh, maybe –" *Come on.* She cleared her throat and tried again. "Maybe it's uh, maybe I-I should give it a miss."

There. Done. Now she could return to her book and pretend this whole day had never happened.

Just as she was about to take a step back, their gazes collided. And all of a sudden everything went quiet. Even her usual, slightly bitchy, inner commentary was silenced. Wade's head dipped and she watched in fascination as his gaze traveled down the length of her. When his eyes dragged back up, her belly clenched. But it didn't feel like her usual anxious stomach ache. No. This felt different. Warmer. No, not warm, hot. Really, really hot.

Something that she didn't recognize flashed in his eyes. "And waste this pretty little dress of yours? I don't think so, petal."

Petal?

His hand was out now, in front of her, palm facing up. It was as if he expected her to hold it.

Surely not? That would be madness.

"Come on, the best man can't be late."

He didn't wait for her to comply; he simply took her hand and ushered her away from the safety of her doorway. Her heart was beating so fast, she was worried for her rib cage. Maybe that was why she followed him. Her body took the lead while her brain was distracted by a possible medical emergency.

DON'T MISS THE REST OF THE BOOKS IN THE LOVE BURNS SERIES

Toasted

Welcome to Woodvalley Pines...where hunky firefighters save the day! It's time to turn up the heat and hope this smokin' hot fireman can control the blaze.

Libby hadn't even been in Woodvalley Pines a day and she was already freaking out. Her kitchen had just set on fire. From toast of all things! That's right, she was the victim of the elusive toaster fire. Yes, a toaster. Who knew they could just spontaneously burst into flames? She certainly didn't. If that wasn't enough to ruin her day, a swarm of hot firefighters seeing her in her pink pajamas would do it.

Zach tried his hardest not to laugh as the woman in the Disney pajamas accused him of keeping toaster fire safety a secret. He didn't know where in the world this angry green-eyed princess had come from, but he had to admit that he was intrigued. After all, if she had this much passion when it came to talking toasters, what other kind of flames could he stoke in her?

Libby and Zach's spark was instant, but will the fire burn out or can they keep the flames blazing?

Isobel Reed's snarky humorous romances have fans fanning themselves as they devour the stories. Her books are one-clicks for readers who love Lori Wilde's - The First Love Cookie Club and Jennifer Ryan's - At Wolf Ranch books. Readers will struggle not to fall for the sexy small town heroes and the sassy women who claim them!

EXCERPT:

"You okay, ma'am? Neighbor reported he heard screaming."

Oh shit.

"Oh, yeah. There was screaming. I mean, yes, I did scream. But it was more like a release, y'know? Like, when you're having a really shitty day and you scream into a pillow. It was kinda like that." *For the love of God, stop talking.* "Anyway, yeah, I'm fine. All good. Hunky-dory."

Hunky-dory? Really? And screaming into pillows? Way to embarrass yourself in front of the handsome firefighters. Are your Disney pajamas not enough humiliation for you? Do you want to detail your hair removal regime next?

Luckily, the other man decided not to comment. He simply nodded, for which Libby was grateful. Once he'd given Zach a quick update on the cause of the fire – that blasted toaster – he disappeared and left the two of them alone again.

Turns out, just the mention of the toaster was enough to bring back her rage.

"Did you know toasters just sometimes set on fire? When exactly did that become a thing? And why aren't there more people talking about it?"

Zach incorrectly thought that clearing his throat would be enough to mask his snigger. "Uh, well, any old appliances can be a potential fire hazard. With toasters, a build-up of breadcrumbs can also act as fuel to the fire."

"What the hell? I didn't know that, Zach. Why didn't I know that? Is this some big firefighter secret or something? 'Cause I'm telling you right now, people need to know this! I'm thirty-one, Zach. *Thirty-one!* And never in my life would I have thought I could be making toast one day and then … *boom!* Fire! People need to be told. They need to know, damnit!"

Okay, it was safe to say this was not her finest moment. She was well aware ranting about toaster fires while sitting on the curb – in just her miniscule, bright pink shorts and vest top – was giving off batshit crazy vibes. But she clearly just couldn't help herself. Once she got a look at his expression, the crazy continued.

"Are you laughing at me?"

"No, ma'am."

"You are … you're laughing at me!"

"Smiling. I'm smiling at you. There's a big difference."

Cop-Off

Return to Woodvalley Pines...where a sexy police officer comes across one troublemaker that he's determined to pin down.

Cat is looking to snag herself a cowboy. After all, what else is there to do in the small town of Woodvalley Pines. And after the year she's had, she deserves to treat herself. There's only one problem. Cody freaking McBride. The devil himself. And the bane of her existence. It's bad enough she has to look at his smug face most days, but now he's made it his mission to meddle in her love life. Which means only one thing, it's about to get ugly.

Single dad and local cop Cody thought he was done with love. He was content in his routine. Work, eat, sleep, repeat. But then Cat shows up in town. Lighting fires wherever she goes and hurling insults his way while she's doing it. He actually finds himself enjoying fighting with the little she-devil, it's the most alive he's felt in years.

Woodvalley Pines is about to witness the ultimate showdown. Where clothes aren't the only things getting torn to shreds.

Cop-Off is set in a small town filled with sassy heroines, hunky heroes, and busybodies who can't help but share their two cents. Fans of Any Man of Mine by Rachel Gibson and Worth the Risk by Jamie Beck will love Isobel Reed's steamy, snarky romance!

EXCERPT:

"You cannot write that!" Libby gasped, handing Cat back her phone.

"Why not?"

"Because you're going to attract the wrong kind of man!"

Why her friend seemed so horrified, Cat had no idea. All she'd done was show her the profile she'd set up on a local dating app. It had been Libby's idea to get back out there in the first place. That was exactly what she was doing.

"Look, Lib, I love you, but you drag me all the way out here to the middle of nowhere to, what, sit around all day? If I'm gonna be surrounded by nothing but cows, I might as well find myself a cowboy to shag."

And she *was* in the middle of nowhere. Woodvalley Pines, Wyoming was a long way from her home in Brighton, England. This hadn't exactly been what she imagined when she'd thought about moving back to America. The last time she was here, she'd been living in San Francisco, where she'd first met Libby. And she had to admit she missed the city. The hustle and bustle. Nights out. Takeout whenever you wanted it. The most exciting thing that had happened since moving to Woodvalley was the day Mrs Tucker lost her cat. For an hour.

"A dating profile full of innuendos is not gonna find you a cowboy. It's gonna find you a horny psychopath." Libby obviously wasn't done yet.

"You're being dramatic."

"Cat, at one point you wrote: *Before I take a long ride, I like to make sure my stud has had a good twenty minute warm up.*" Her best friend's eyebrow was raised, causing her to look all accusatory.

"What?" Cat not-so-innocently lifted her bare shoulder in a shrug. "That's just good horsemanship, Lib. You don't want him to be too stiff." She added a wink specifically to get a laugh out of her. And it worked.

Baked

When danger comes to the small town of Woodvalley Pines, Hunter vows to become the protector of local bakery owner, Rachel. But when things heat up, can this firefighter handle the burn?

Rachel was finally happy. She had a place to call home, amazing friends, and a successful bakery. Then her past found her. Now Hunter Campbell was in her kitchen, acting like a caveman. After months of only grunting at her, one little incident, and he has the audacity to tell her she's not allowed out without him. She couldn't decide what terrified her more about her new bodyguard – the giant hulk scaring off her customers, or the fire in her belly that made her heart race every time he was near.

Local firefighter Hunter was a man of few words. But if ever there was a time to talk, it was now. Rachel was in danger and there was no way he was going to let anything happen to his stubborn little fairy. It didn't matter that he'd spent months keeping his distance. Or that she had the power to shatter his heart and then stab him to death with the shards. This was happening. She could bang as many baking pans as she liked. He wasn't going anywhere. She was stuck with him.

Fighting fires was nothing new to Rachel or Hunter, but surrendering to the heat of the flames was a battle neither of them were prepared for.

Isobel Reed's stories delight and bring laughter to romance through sizzling dialogue and fast-paced writing. Fans of Hot Stuff by Carly Phillips or Rescue Me by Susan May Warren will love this sassy tale of a caveman fireman and the baker who wins his heart.

EXCERPT:

Striding down the terracotta cobbles like a man on a mission, Hunter knew what most people saw as they crossed the street to avoid him. But just because most people compared his physical build to the Hulk, it didn't mean he also had the whole wrath thing going on too. Although, if he was ever going to suddenly develop anger issues, this week would have done it.

He was pissed as hell. Nine months he'd stayed away. Kept his distance. Damn well tortured himself. And all for nothing. Because now? Now he didn't have a choice. There would be no staying away anymore. Not while Rachel was in danger. It changed everything.

What kind of man would he be if he let something happen to the woman he'd not been able to stop thinking about since he first laid eyes on her, just because he couldn't get over himself?

A shit one.

Exactly. He was fine being many things. A man of few words. A man most people had to stretch their necks to see fully. He was even fine being a man who tipped the loneliness scale a bit too enthusiastically. But he drew the line at being a shit one.

That being said, he knew what going to her meant. He wasn't dense. There had been a reason he'd stayed away. A good one. And now he was willingly throwing himself into the fire.

It meant he was done running. Done fighting his feelings. It was time to claim his honeybun. It was time to claim Rachel. And that's exactly what he was on his way to do.

Stopping outside the pastel pink storefront, his eyes went to the even pinker neon sign that hung above the window display. The name Fairy Baked was flashing above a line of pretty cupcakes that had been sprinkled with assorted candy.

You've got this. Just go inside and calmly explain that starting from today, she is not to go anywhere without an escort.

Easy.

AVAILABLE IN EBOOK AND PRINT WHERE BOOKS ARE SOLD

ABOUT THE AUTHOR

Isobel was born and raised in London. While she's a city girl at heart, she loves daydreaming about running away to a charming small town—though she's not entirely sure her husband and son would share her enthusiasm for the move. When she's not writing small-town romantic comedies or growing unhealthily attached to the characters in her books, you can find her reading, chasing after her very active toddler, or attempting to channel her inner domestic goddess in the kitchen (with varying degrees of success).

Known for her witty dialogue and swoon-worthy small-town heroes, Isobel signed with Inkspell Publishing in 2021. The following year, she released Love Tools, the first book in her four-book Bluestone Series. In early 2024, she launched Toasted, the debut novel of her seven-book Love Burns Series, which will roll out over the next year.

https://www.tiktok.com/@isobelreedbooks
https://www.facebook.com/isobelreedbooks
https://www.instagram.com/isobelreedbooks/
https://www.isobelreed.net/
https://www.amazon.com/author/isobelreed
https://www.goodreads.com/Isobel_Reed
https://www.bookbub.com/authors/isobel-reed

www.ingramcontent.com/pod-product-compliance
Lightning Source LLC
Chambersburg PA
CBHW020120180626
46812CB00006B/2679